EDWARD'S CAT

A MAGICAL TALE OF EDWARD, HIS TWIN AND A CAT

MARIA P FRINO

MPG COMMUNICATIONS

DEDICATION

To my writing group friends, Write On Water
You inspire my writing with every meeting

COPYRIGHT

Maria P Frino

First published in 2023. © Maria P. Frino, 2023 The moral rights of the author have been asserted. All rights reserved. Except as permitted under the Australian Copyright Act 1968 (for example, a fair dealing for the purposes of study, research, criticism or review), no part of this book may be reproduced, stored in a retrieval system, communicated or transmitted in any form or by any means without prior written permission.

This is a work of fiction.

Title: Edward's Cat– a novella
Author: Maria P. Frino

Cover Design: Mark Drolc - http://onthemarkdesign. com.au/

Visit the author's website at www.mariapfrino.com

All inquiries should be made to the author - mariapfrino@gmail.com

ONE

Edward
and Milly the Cat

High atop a bough of our Jacaranda tree I peer over to the Pacific in all its majestic glory. The blue mesmerises me along with the purple flowers of the Jacaranda. Our tree is in full bloom, the blossoms infusing it in a spectacular purple. Other Jacarandas have our neighbourhood flooded in a sea of purple wherever I look. The red roofs are peppered through the Jacarandas of our seaside suburb, a middle-class haven on Sydney's northern beaches.

This is my favourite spot, my shelter, away from everyone and since summer school holidays are only a few weeks away, I will spend most of my time here. As I sit, I can smell the sweet scents of jasmine and murraya coming from the gardens surrounding my home. The pungency of the smells soothe me.

The sky is breaking blue as the sun rises over the ocean. I feel the warmth seeping through me. Today will be warm. I contemplate what this day will bring. Will it be peaceful with everyone leaving me alone? Will I be tormented? Or will the bullies find someone else to taunt?

"Milly, come on down. It's time for breakfast."

That's Mum. She always knows I'm up here when I need time alone. And this morning she calls me by my cat name. I while away hours up here, but not today. Unfortunately, school beckons. I hesitate not wanting to leave the peace that envelopes me. This sanctuary feeds my soul, I am my best self when I sit on this bough. I am safe, why do I have to leave?

"Edward, did you hear me?"

Oh, she's angry now because I didn't respond. When she calls me by my human name, I know it's time to move. With a huge cat stretch, I pounce from branch to branch until I hit the ground on all fours. As I head towards our house, the process of metamorphosis now allows me to walk on two legs. I'm Edward again and I'm a shape shifter.

Walking over to the breakfast bench, she acknowledges me. I nod but stay mute. Mum knows me too well. She has a sixth sense of when I want to share and when I don't. Since my sister… I still find it hard to think of her not being here. I miss her sitting next to me, taunting me in her sisterly manner. She's gone and has been for a year. Still, it is no easier to live without her.

The school playground is alive with young, eager students, all milling around waiting for assembly. I'm in my corner swamped in a sea of discarded purple petals under a huge Jacaranda, away from everyone. No one wants to talk to someone like me. I'm different and being different at St Scholastica's is taboo. Tall for my age, my body is disproportionate to my head, which is yet to grow into my body. My eyes, beady, brown and boring. Teeth that protrude over my bottom lip, the braces helping but not fast enough. And let's not talk about my hair, long strands of thin nothingness in mousy brown. If my skin wasn't so white, I'd be one whole lot of brown.

I see them heading towards me, Chase and his cronies. *Do it now Milly. Transform me now!* This would be the easiest way to escape the torment they are about to thrust upon me, but I cannot control when I am able to perform my metamorphosis. It was my sister Milly who had the ability to transform at will and since her death I have unwittingly been bestowed the power, though not at will. This is a slight inhibitor to me being able to use it when necessary.

Chase is well-known as the school bully and also for being a bit dim. He struts his stuff perfectly well as an athlete, especially on the football field and the basketball court, but as a student, he is challenged. I have to hold my tongue whenever Chase tries to sound more intelligent than he is. Little does he know that all his victims laugh at him behind his back, it's their only form of revenge. Me, I picture him as a clown, this helps me to handle what is going to happen next.

I run towards the oval, but they easily catch up. Chase is a bully in the ilk of Voldemort, the difference being Chase is real and standing in front of me. Being the same height, we can eye each other. Chase is flanked by Morgan, Shane and Chase's sometime girlfriend, Brooke. Why she bothers is beyond me. It's obviously his looks. He towers over everyone in our year. Blonde locks scatter down his forehead and over his ears. His charcoal grey eyes pour fear over anyone who bothers him. The only thing missing for Chase is a brain. He is a sports hero but academically he has no hope. Brooke is a smart girl, an A-grade student actually…and a cute brunette. *Why Chase?*

To give you an idea of how Chase and Brooke are opposites, here's an anecdote of a time when Chase really showed his stupidity. Assembly was dragging on this particular day and I overheard Chase whispering to Brooke about what a dickhead the headmaster is. Brooke whispers back that he is being obnoxious and Chase, without a beat says, "What do you mean? I'm not obnochous." I had to do everything in my power not to laugh out loud and I'm imagining Brooke wondering why he bothers with words he knows nothing about, let alone pronounce.

I am still musing over this point when Chase booms at his cavemen friends, Morgan and Shane to pick me up. With each of them holding me by my underarms, my feet dangling, Chase, with his fists clenched, spells out what he will do to me. The others snigger at what he is spurting out. When he finishes his rant, he says, "I'm feeling particularly annoyed at you today, Eddie."

I cringe at him calling me by this shortened version of my name. Telling him *sotto voce* my name is Edward only infuriates him further.

"Couldn't give a rat's arse you little piece of shit. Now, I want to know how you disappeared from sight last Friday afternoon. One minute I had you gripped by the shirt, the next my clenched hand was holding onto nothing. We all know you're different, you fat-arsed weasel, but this vanishing trick you've perfected, tell me how you do it?"

I have transformed at various times at school, mostly for no reason at all. Stress can bring on a transformation, maybe that was what caused me to transform on what was a particularly bad day. Chase did provoke me mercilessly that day.

I am willing myself to transform now, why can't I make it happen? Especially when I need it like… right now! My underarms ache as I glare at the two cavemen, Morgan and Shane. Why hasn't the assembly bell gone yet? "I don't know what you're talking about?" I answer Chase enslaved by the pain.

"Don't play dumb with us Eddie. Tell us how you do it and we'll let you go."

I remain stubborn. Partly because I don't know what to tell them and partly because I wouldn't tell them even if I knew how the transforming works. Milly and I didn't discuss how she did it. It was a power she was born with. As her twin, why I wasn't bestowed the same blessing at birth annoys the hell out of me.

The assembly bell chimes.

"Shit! Put him down, we'll deal with this at lunch time. You've a few hours to think about this Eddie. If I were you, I'd reveal your secret to avoid some broken ribs."

I head towards my class line. Year 6 stands towards the back of the quadrangle but next year we will be moving onto high school. Will high school be any different? For the geeks of this school like me. I don't think so.

The day drags on, I'm feeling frustrated with these boring lessons and just want to be home.

TWO

Bullies Beware

My room's musty pre-teen smell soothes my nerves. My ribs ache, although they are not broken. They were damaged after another visit from Chase. The teacher intervening halfway through the bashing, helped. Chase and his cronies were given detention. I feel some pleasure from this, but it is not enough to stop Chase. He'll keep bullying me until my last day of school.

As I worry, I'm suddenly on the bough of the Jacaranda. Becoming Milly means no pain, her cat ribs are not damaged. The bliss of being agile and able to move without pain is wonderful. What time is it? I hope I won't be here for long, even though I do want to stay. I'm starving, my stomach growls like a lion on the prowl. Chase was upon me as I was about to eat my sandwich at lunchtime. He took the remainder of my lunch with him.

As I contemplate the horizon, I realise Chase is allergic to cats. "Those mangy animals," he has let everyone know. His disdain for cats will be an asset for Milly. It's time to pay him a visit. With this thought, I pounce down and pad my way to Chase's house on the hill.

Arriving at their front door, I hear him speaking to his mother. He speaks to her in the same churlish tone he uses with everyone. He has no respect for anyone, it is all about Chase. They have a dog, I can't remember what type, but it means I can enter through the pet door. I slink my way in, taking in the smells. Part human sweat, part dog hormones and part some type of sickly air freshener.

Their dog, a Pekinese with a pink ribbon atop her head, is suddenly in front of me snarling in the wimpiest growl. I'm laughing and wonder whether Milly's face conveys this. Probably not as the snarl doesn't change.

"Buttercup what's going on? What's all this noise?" *Buttercup. Yeah, that's an appropriate name.* Chase's mother comes looking. "Oh, hello. Where did you come from? You are very cute, but you can't stay here, my son is allergic. Come on out you go."

I swerve past her with ease and sniff out where Chase is. Finding him in his room, which is twice the size of mine, Chase starts sneezing and scratching the minute I jump onto his lap and pee.

"What the… get off me. How the hell did you get in here. Mum throw this disgusting thing out of our house. And bring me my antihistamines," he yells.

Buttercup is now barking as I hiss at her while running past heading towards the pet door. Milly's job here is done.

As I run through the pet door, I transform. The pain sears through me and I instinctively place pressure to the injury with my hand. It soothes the area a little. This agony is going to slow me down, but that's not a problem, I have given Chase a dose of his own medicine. Direct contact with a cat means he will be scratching for days. My face beams with pleasure as I amble home.

I'm back in my room before my parents are home, there is

no need for them to know where I have gone. In fact, they won't even need to know I went out today other than going to school. *Thanks Milly, your timing was perfect. How many times have I tried to think of how to hurt Chase as much as he has hurt me over the years?* In the end, you're there for me. Now, if only she would help me control the transformations. Chase is going to be angry and ready to burst out at anyone who is in his way. I desperately want to hurt him again, this time by leaving a few scratches that will fester.

It's Friday and assembly goes on longer this morning because the principal is giving a lecture on bullying. *How appropriate.* Has someone informed him about Chase? I wonder how many kids at this school are being bullied that has prompted the principal to discuss the issue this time? There are murmurs throughout the assembly, probably from the lucky ones who don't have to deal with this problem. My insides burn as this authority figure spurts out the usual trite about being nice to each other, about tolerance and appreciating each other's differences. *Oh yeah, that's exactly what the bully is thinking while pummelling me.*

Finally, we're in class and I notice Chase is missing. It's with glee I see his empty chair in the back corner. Today is going to be a good day.

I'm walking out of science class when I bump into Morgan and Shane. "Hey, you fat-arse weasel, watch where you're going." Morgan's booming voice rattles me as he mimics Chase. Morgan doesn't have a speaking voice, no matter what comes out of his mouth, it is a shout. I ignore him.

The next class is a double maths lesson. My favourite lesson and I'm happy when a substitute teacher is taking the class. She hands out some papers asking us to work on them. Easy. This means I can smash through these and relax on my phone. Can this day get any better?

Shane, who is sitting behind me, is whispering to Morgan about Chase. "He's in a bad way, apparently, he's scratching so much, his skin is red raw and bleeding. He isn't coming back to school until next week. He's in too much pain."

"Poor guy. He suffers badly from this cat allergy. We'll go over after school and cheer him up."

"Yep, good idea."

This day is the best day of my school life. I managed to maim the great Chase Richardson enough to stop him coming to school for the next week. This means a whole week of no bullying for me and any of the other geeks he picks on. *Milly, when you're ready I'll be waiting to give that jerk another dose of your medicine. I'm ready for a lot more of these types of adventures.* This day is a win for all of us who are bullied and are too scared to give the arseholes a dose of their own treatment.

As I walk home from school, I have a new-found strength and relish in the knowledge that Milly has my back. I miss my twin with all my heart, never feeling whole now she is gone. But with this gift she has bestowed me, that of transforming, she is always with me. This will help me to navigate life without fear of bullies like Chase and his species.

THREE

Afternoon Snacks

The sun is beating down as we wait in line to buy an afternoon snack at the local fish 'n' chip shop. I see Morgan and Shane pushing in front of a group of Year 3 boys. "Arseholes," I mutter under my breath. One of the boys tries to protest and is physically grabbed by both bullies and told to "shut his trap." I hear the boy whimpering as he is unceremoniously pushed behind the other Year 3 boys.

When I eventually buy my hot chips, I scoff them down, burning my fingers. They are crisp and salty. My mouth is savouring every chip.

"Something needs to be done about those bullies. What they're doing sucks."

I turn to see Trudi who is also a geek at our school. Like me she is bullied by Chase and his cronies. Trudi wears glasses so is spared some of the physical taunts, but she is targeted with vicious words. Quietly spoken, smart and lanky in a giraffe-like way, makes her a target like me. We're different. No one talks about our looks like the popular kids, whose appearance is all they have. Well mostly, Brooke is an exception. "Hi. Umm, pardon? I was throwing my chip packet away and didn't hear you."

"We need to do something about the bullying. That assembly was a joke, as if the bullies listen to all that rubbish."

I nod and invite Trudi to walk with me. She lives near my place, and we do occasionally walk home together. Looking up at her, I say, "Yeah, I'm sick of their crap. Do you have a suggestion?" She remains quiet for a bit. I guess she is mulling her ideas over. I'm not ready to discuss Milly's adventures with her yet. I listen to what she has to say.

"Maybe we should gang up with the other victims and show them that we won't take their taunts anymore."

"Everyone is so scared of them; they would need some convincing. We would have to give assurances for their safety. As much as what is happening sucks, all our safety comes first."

"That's true. But the way things are none of us is safe."

We continue walking as we discuss ideas until I arrive at my front gate. "Good chat Trudi, maybe we should discuss our ideas with other victims and see if we can change things at school. By the way, which high school are you going to?"

"I'd like to see a change at all schools, but that's a pipe dream. Redman High, you?"

"I'm going to Redman too. Great, then we can keep discussing things and make changes at both schools. See you around, Trudi."

"Ok, see you," says Trudi as she trudges down the street.

Trudi is considered a geek because she always has a book with her and usually has her nose in it. She is one of the smart ones, who like me just doesn't fit in with the *it* crowd. I like her and her unruly dark brown curls. She is stick-thin even though I've seen her eat as much as any of the boys and we have enjoyed lots of fish 'n' chips after school. I'm happy we're going to be at the same high school, it will make what we want to do about the bullies that much easier.

Walking inside, I head to the kitchen for a long, cold drink. The salty chips and talking with Trudi have left me thirsty, my tongue feeling like furry fuzz. Maybe I should tell Trudi about Milly and how she's helping me? Would she believe me? *Hmm, this needs more investigation.*

The next morning, I wake up early with a fantastic idea. When I transform again, I'll visit Trudi's house and check out whether she is a cat person. If she is, then I'll tell her what's happening and together we can fight those bullies. Even though Trudi only lives a street away, we've never visited each other's homes. It's time we became better friends.

Ants march like little trojans, the cracks on the sidewalk not bothering them. It's amazing what I notice when I transform into Milly. Being closer to the ground there are so many details we miss as humans. I sniff at the grass and ants tickle my nose. *Arr…choo.* Rubbing my nose with my paw I continue onto Trudi's house. It's been a week since we spoke outside the fish shop, and I've been waiting to metamorphosise into Milly. Today is the day to do some research on Trudi.

Arriving at the picket fence, I pounce over it. The front yard is immaculate with roses lining one fence while other colourful flowers I don't know the names of line the picket fence. My nose takes in all the summery smell the flowers emit. It's pleasant and I enjoy this as I walk towards the front door. There are various shoes strewn on the porch and a bowl with water as well. I sniff it but don't drink because it smells like it's been there for days. I keep sniffing around and know there is another cat on the other side of the door. I hear it sniffing too, then I hear… "meeeooow", a long and low one. I remain quiet.

The door opens and Trudi looks down, "Oh, hello. Where

did you come from? I know most of the cats in this area, but who are you?"

I rub myself over her bare feet and ankles. She laughs, "You're a friendly one aren't you."

Standing by the open door is the other cat, his back arching and he's hissing at me.

"Don't be so rude, Casper, this lovely ginger has come to say hello." Trudi bends down to pat my head and whispers, "Where do you live? I hope you know your way home." She checks my neck where my collar should be. "Hmm, no collar but you don't look like a stray."

Casper decides to ignore me and pads back into the house. Well at least I know that Trudi is a cat person, this research has been successful.

FOUR

An Afternoon Stroll

One minute I'm sitting in English class, the next I'm on the branch of the Jacaranda tree. It's the Tuesday of the week Chase is away, maybe this is another perfect opportunity to pay him a visit. But Milly has other ideas. As I pounce down onto the ground, I turn the opposite way from Chase's place. I guess it's a nice afternoon for a stroll because it's not too hot, but this time I have no idea where I'm headed. It's almost as if Milly has taken over my mind.

I walk through the local streets I know so well. Walk past the homes where my classmates live and walk past some local shops all adorned in Christmas splendour. Doesn't anyone notice this ginger cat strolling along by herself? Apparently not because no one is looking at me and wondering why there is a cat in the local shopping strip. Can anyone see me? Am I invisible?

The answer to that question is obvious when a little girl holding her mother's hand almost steps on me. She trips but doesn't fall because her mother manages to hold her up. "Whoopsie daisy, what happened there, Lila?"

"I don't know mummy. My foot hit something."

The mother looks around, "There is nothing there, no rubbish and no crack in the concrete to trip you up. Never mind darling, you didn't hurt yourself, let's keep going."

Lila smiles at her mother and they go about their business oblivious of the fact a ginger cat is watching them. *"Wow, how cool is this. I'm invisible. This is another power Milly didn't talk about. Oh, the things I can do to Chase and no-one will know. But why am I walking even further away from his house? I am supposed to be paying him a visit."*

I keep walking and check a couple of the shops by sticking my head in. The florist shop makes me sneeze and I look towards the lady making up a bouquet. No, she doesn't hear anything, I am invisible and can't be heard. *So cool.* Nothing interesting here, so I move on. I'm curious to see where Milly is leading me, what could be so important for a cat to see here at the shops?

Boredom is setting in and wish I could transform back and be in my classroom, but then I see him. It's Chase and he's coming out of the pharmacy.

I run towards him and see he is on his own. I place myself right next to his feet and we walk in unison. He starts rubbing his nose, then pulls out a few tissues from the pharmacy bag. He blows his nose, which is so loud it sounds like a flugelhorn and the people walking in front of him turn around. "What are you gawking at? I'm blowing my nose," he yells at them. They quickly scurry away, as one of them, the tallest boy, gives him the finger.

"Hehe," I laugh, "I'm already making him uncomfortable. This allergy he has is making it so easy for me to exact my revenge again."

In a flash, I'm back in class. Looking around, everyone

including our teacher, is oblivious that I even left. Well, this is very interesting… I can disappear and come back without anyone noticing… and as Milly, I'm invisible sometimes. Oh, the potential. I wonder how many victims of bullies I can help when I'm invisible Milly?

FIVE

Milly
The Human

There is a before and after. Before cancer I was a nine-year-old doing everyday things – school, homework, fighting with my twin brother, magically turning into a cat. You know – normal stuff.

After cancer sucks. Since my diagnosis of brain cancer, I have had multiple tests, many specialist visits and surgery. The treatment is sometimes worse than the actual disease. Throwing up is the worst, but the hardest thing is watching how it affects my Mum and brother, especially since Dad died of lung cancer when Edward and I were only five.

We were coping reasonably well after we lost our father. Mum began working again as a nurse and Edward and I looked after each other as best we could. My mother's sadness permeated the house for the first year, then she became herself again once she was working. Her work gave her purpose and seeing her happy made us happy.

I hurl into the wash basin that is on a chair beside my bed.

Edward has the washer ready for me to wipe my face. He never comments or makes snide remarks about the smell, he just picks up the basin and goes to the laundry to clean it up. Placing the basin back on the chair he sits on the edge of my bed, "What shall we do? Are you feeling ok to go for a walk?"

The sunshine is beaming through the sheer curtains as I look outside, "Sure, let's see if we can walk further than the end of the street today."

Edward smiles as he helps me into the wheelchair.

Oh, you thought I could walk. No, I'm too weak now and my balance is off due to the tumour, which is rearing its ugly head again. Ha, see what I did there? I have brain cancer and that is my attempt at a weak joke. I try to keep my spirits up more for Mum and Edward, they worry enough as it is.

As Edward steers the wheelchair down the ramp onto our driveway, I feel the warmth of the mid-morning sun on my skin. Spring is my favourite time of year and soon the Jacarandas will be in full bloom, with the promise of summer not far away. I was always able to shape shift better in summer than winter, I'm not sure why, maybe cats prefer the heat? Right now, I'm Milly the human, Milly the cat is dormant and I presume its due to the tumour. I miss being a cat and chasing around with the other cats in our neighbourhood. Cancer sucks.

Edward is quiet as he pushes me along. We still fight occasionally, but mostly we are quiet when it's just us. We never speak of me dying, but we know it's there in the background waiting to pounce. It's not long before I tire and we have to go back home. My head hurts more when I'm sitting, so our walks are never long enough. Edward turns back as we hit the end of our street. The same distance as yesterday.

SIX

Edward
    The Big Secret

"You miss her."

It's three months since Milly's funeral and Trudi is walking with me to school. The school year started on the hottest February day with everyone looking forward to the cooler days coming.

"Yes." The word chokes in my throat. I clear it and continue, "Thanks for coming to the funeral." I choke up again, "she liked you," I manage to say.

"Your sister was lovely, we talked and laughed a lot."

We continue walking in silence, the kind of silence that weighs heavy with unsaid words. I had heard many platitudes since Milly's death so am happy to remain silent. All those well-meaning words helped for a minute, but generally they are useless against this long-term agony Mum and I are going through. Mum is so sad she is a shadow of her former self. Having conquered the grief of losing her husband and moving on with life, now she has lost her daughter. My grief is black and ominous, I can't imagine what my mother is feeling.

Entering the main gates of school, Trudi heads to her locker area as I walk to mine. "See you around. If you need to talk, I'm here." I nod towards her giving a meek smile. Of all my *'friends'*, of which I have none, Trudi is the one I know I can count on. How sad that I have only one friend, but at least she is trustworthy.

As I open my locker, I feel the looks of pity from the other students. Many didn't know Milly, but everyone knows she has gone. Her illness had been the talk around town since she was diagnosed. I pay them no notice, I want to be alone and let my feelings tear through this abhorrent grief.

The first week of school is the hardest with everyone giving me looks and whispering as I walk past. This is my last year at this school and I can't wait to leave. Hopefully, Chase and his bullies won't be going to Redman High. It's also hard because I am battling the grief of losing my twin. This is the torture of grief, it grips you and is relentless. I actually thought it would be easier this time having already lost our father, but it's worse. Milly was my twin, I've lost my other half. I put my head down so no one sees my tears as I wipe snot from my nose. Cancer sucks.

After months of torture at the hands of Chase, I've had enough. I've been thinking about telling Trudi about how I transform and now is the time. This is the moment I decide to tell her.

We're walking home after school when I say, "Trudi, I have something to tell you."

She looks at my face and knows it's something serious. Without missing a beat she says, "I'm listening."

"Before I tell you, promise me you won't laugh, ridicule me or tell others?" She nods with an inquisitive look on her face. I proceed to tell her my secret feeling somewhat nervous and scared. I tell her how my sister had a magic power and when she died, it was transferred to me. *Well, almost all of her power*.

"Holy hell, that is some story. And by the look on your face, it's true."

"Of course, it's true. Why would I make something like this up? I've been wanting to tell you for ages but I was scared you would think I'm crazy. And now I can see that you do."

Trudi places her hand on my arm indicating I stop walking. She turns to me, "I don't think you're crazy, you're the most together guy I know, but this story…it takes some getting used to. I'm trying to process what you've told me, I mean, what, err…how do you do it?"

"I'm the *'most together guy'* you know? Trudi, I'm the only guy you know." I laugh and she along with me. "Do you have other guy friends?" She scoffs and I continue, "How would I know what you said to the ginger cat that came to your house? I know because I am the ginger cat. I can transform into that cat. And I don't know how it happens, Milly took all that knowledge with her." Trudi is shuffling her feet, looking at my face then turning away. Have I done the right thing? Maybe I should have kept the secret to myself and just kept it within my family.

"Holy shit, that's fantastic. So, you're the one who kept Chase away from school for a week. I love it." Trudi keeps talking and I can't get a word in. Her enthusiasm is great but she isn't giving me time to speak. I want to make sure she isn't going to tell anyone about this.

When she finally stops, I say, "Ok, thanks Trudi, I'm pleased you're happy. But you have to assure me you will not tell anyone else, I have trusted you with a huge secret that only my Mum and I know."

"Absolutely, you have my word. But, wow, I'm blown away. Amazing, that is some power you have there, Edward."

"An uncontrollable power, but yes, it is a power I can use.

Now, we have to ask the other geeks to meet us after school one day to discuss our plan. I was thinking during the spring holidays, we could meet at the park opposite your place."

"Absolutely, let's do it. I'll send text messages to the kids I know, you do the same. This is so cool, we're going to beat the bullies at their own game."

"Ah, I don't know about beating them, but we can give them a scare, that's for sure." We keep walking home and I again ask her not to tell anyone.

"It's between us and your Mum. No one else will ever know, I promise *again*." She looks at me with a stern look telling me I'm not to mess with her, she has my back. "See you tomorrow, Edward and try to stop worrying."

I watch as she keeps walking towards her street and hope like hell she means what she is saying.

Two weeks later we meet with twenty other bullied students at the park. After telling them what we're here for, they are all onboard with the idea of standing up to the bullies. They tell us there are more geeks being bullied but they didn't want to be involved, they're too scared.

"It's ok, twenty of you plus us two is a massive number. We can do some damage by being aware when someone is being bullied and we assist as a group. Obviously, we need numbers to make the bullies understand we mean business, don't intervene unless there are at least eight of us. There is safety in numbers."

They agree if we all stick together this may work. I don't mention Milly the cat because they don't have to know. Trudi is the only person other than my mum that I trust with my secret.

SEVEN

Redman High
    The Year of the Geeks

I say goodbye to Trudi as she heads to her locker. We're only in one class together, science, which is fine because we hang out during recess and lunch. Ever since I told her about how I can transform, our friendship has grown stronger. "That is so cool," she had said amongst other things, "I knew there was something special about that ginger cat at my door."

I had laughed out loud, "How could you know? I look like a normal ginger cat."

"Just a feeling, that's all. When I checked for a collar, I knew you weren't a stray, you were too healthy. Ooh, I can't wait to help you with your adventures, I'm sure there will be more bullies to deal with at high school."

Along with the other geeks, Trudi and I had spent most of the last months of primary school and the summer holidays together. The other kids who had met us at the park were now part of our circle, especially when we had to rescue one of them from being bullied. This is how we kept each other safe. Whenever we noticed someone being harassed by Chase, a few of us would gang up on him. Not even Morgan or Shane was a match when the geeks came out in force.

Trudi and I were amazed when fifteen of the geeks followed us to Redman High. We still had safety in numbers.

Although Chase and his cronies bullied Trudi and I in primary, we both felt stronger for having the other geeks around and because we knew that at times, Milly the cat would come to our rescue. The anger I felt was probably the catalyst to help me transform only days after each torment. Trudi and I relished in being able to avenge ourselves with Milly terrorising not only Chase but also Morgan and Shane. Other kids were wondering where this cat was coming from but secretly, they enjoyed seeing the bullies suffer. Morgan and Shane weren't allergic, they only received a ghastly fright from Milly along with some brutal scratches. Chase vowed to find this cat and take it to the pound because no one was owning up as its owner. The hilarity of all his and his cronies' remonstrations kept Trudi and I going for the rest of our last year at primary. These bullies didn't follow us to Redman High but we knew there were more of their ilk at this new school. It wasn't long before they found us.

The afternoon bell rings as everyone begins shuffling to lockers, buses and to head home on foot. I meet Trudi at her locker and we are about to walk to the gate when…

"Not so fast you two weasels." It was Buster. *I know, a stupid name but that's what everyone calls him.* His real name is Noel, which he hates and never uses.

We turn to see him with Jackson, Willow and Isla. The *Gang* as they're known, they are the main bullies of the school, there are two other groups but they are rivals to these guys.

Trudi and I stare at them as my insides begin to feel the queasiness I always feel when a confrontation is imminent.

"We haven't got 'round to youse yet." I cringe at Buster's

drawl and his lack of verbal skills. "We'd like to introduce ourselves, me, I'm Buster… and you don't mess with me." He points to his chest. "These guys," he gestures to the three others standing next to him, "are my gang. Don't be stupid arses with them either. This is my main man, Jackson, and the girls – Willow and Isla." Jackson puffs out his chest and the girls' faces are stern. "Now, we've heard a rumour you like to disappear without warning, Eddie."

"My name is Edward." I say this with anger, my voice raising a notch.

"Don't interrupt when I'm talking you shithead. I'll call you whatever the bloody hell I want to. And that goes for your girlfriend too."

"She's not…"

"What the fuck! Didn't I tell you not to interrupt me?" With that he is up against my face and punches me in the gut.

"Hey," yells Trudi. I scowl at her from my bent over position willing her not to become involved.

Buster is about to yell back at Trudi when a teacher calls from the end of the hall. "What's going on here? It's time you all went home." It's our science teacher.

"Yes, Mr Ferris. We were sayin' goodbye to our friends. See ya tomorrow, Mr Ferris." Buster says this without missing a beat. He went from brute to angelic student in a split second.

Trudi bends down to make sure I'm ok as they leave. Mr Ferris comes to check on my condition. "Did something happen here?"

Trudi lies for us both, "No, Sir. Edward has a tummy ache, that's all. I'll get him home safely."

"Ok, be off then. The bell went fifteen minutes ago."

"Yes, Sir." Trudi takes my arm and leads me towards the front gate. "That was close. We need to keep our mouths shut around Buster from now on."

I stand up straighter now, the pain has subsided. "All it

took is one week, that's all. We're already being bullied at this school."

"Yeah it sucks, I know of a few kids who were bullied on the first day, so we're lucky I guess. Come on, let's get you home."

EIGHT

The Gang

A few days later I am on the bough of the Jacaranda tree, the last golden rays of the sun behind me. This is the first time I've transformed since starting high school. It seems the pattern that started in primary is continuing, I transform one or two days after being bullied. It's too early to begin avenging us geeks yet, Trudi and I don't know enough about this new set of bullies. Looks like we're targeted by Buster and his gang, so we need to research what they're all about before attacking.

"Milly, come down, dinner's ready." It's Mum calling me. She knows I like being called by my cat name when I'm transformed, it makes me feel closer to my sister. I pounce down each branch until I hit the ground. As I walk towards our back deck, I'm back to being Edward and thinking about calling Trudi to discuss researching the Gang.

Sitting at the dinner table, I notice Mum is unusually quiet and somewhat frazzled. "Are you ok? Did something happen today?"

She rubs her hand through her hair, sighing. "Nothing more than usual. The patients are challenging as always, I'm tired I guess." Her job as an aged care nurse takes its toll on her, but more so now Milly has gone. Death is part of what happens in her line of work. "Thanks for asking, Edward. And thanks for noticing, most kids your age wouldn't have a clue how their parents are feeling."

"Mum, it's only you and me now, of course I notice. Why don't you do something special for yourself, a massage maybe?"

"You're sweet but money is tight."

"I can help by getting a job. A paper run maybe?"

"Does that job still exist? Doesn't everyone read the papers online?"

"Good point. You know what I mean though, let me help out, I'm old enough."

"Not quite, I think you have to be fifteen before you can work. Please don't worry, I'm fine. Nothing a bit of rest won't fix." I sense she doesn't want to continue this discussion and go back to eating the schnitzel she prepared.

It's Saturday morning and Trudi and I are in my bedroom. I have my laptop with all the socials open. We're stalking the Gang and the girls are the easiest to find, they're on all of them. Willow and Isla are cousins, their birthdays are the same date a month apart. Neither has siblings.

"They have that in common with me, but that's about it. Especially in the looks department, these two look like barbie dolls with their blonde locks, huge eyes, excessive makeup and killer nails," says Trudi

"Yeah, what is it with the nails. Why so long?"

"It's an *it-girl* thing. Besides, with their rich parents, their allowance gives them privileges we mere mortals don't have."

I snort at that, "We are mere mortals compared to them."

Next, we find Buster's profile. Nowhere is his real name, Noel Sterling, to be found. He goes under Buster Sterlz. "This guy is a wanker. He's even changed his last name."

"I've heard he hates his stepdad and refuses to take his last name too. From what I hear his stepdad shouldn't be messed with. Apparently, his real dad wasn't much better."

"Ah, now we know where Buster gets it from. And what about Jackson?"

"Here, look. He's using his real name, Jackson Walker. You know, from his profile I wonder what he's doing hanging around with Buster? He's the eldest of three brothers, all of whom are doing well."

"I know, he doesn't strike me as a jerk like Buster. We'll have to do more digging on him."

We continue for hours finding out as much information as possible on all of them. Buster's weak link is how dumb he is, Jackson is trying to fit in after moving schools a few times, and the girls just want to be part of the *it crowd*. Their photos show they are part of a few groups, all girls following alpha males and all of them posting way too many selfies with different guys. Aren't these girls worried about their reputation?

Trudi answers, "Do you think they care?"

"Did I say that out loud? And yes, I do think they will care one day. This will come back to bite them."

"What about the boys? Don't they have reputations to uphold?"

I realise how sexist I sounded, "Shit, you're right. It's not just the girls that should worry." I think about what I said so flippantly. It is sad that girls have to protect their reputation, which is harder to do these days because social media has seen to that. I guess girls don't worry too much about their reputation now because the playing field is levelled to the point where it doesn't matter. Still, as with me, I think boys still see girls as the fairer sex meaning that a good reputation does count.

Trudi looks at her phone. "I gotta go, it's after one, my parents will want me to clean my room. It's a Saturday ritual at my place, cleaning the house. Besides, I think we have enough info, so see you at school on Monday," she says standing and heading towards the door.

"Yeah, see you then. We can work out what to do at the next meeting with the other geeks."

Buster is behind Edward in the canteen queue. "Hey, shithead, move." He whispers this into my ear as I cringe at his stale smoker's breath. Not cigarette breath though, he's stoned and it's only mid-morning.

I move behind him without answering.

"Na, the end of the line. Now!" This is yelled at the top of his lungs making everyone jump.

One of the ladies behind the canteen counter reprimands Buster but I do as I'm told. I'm not in the mood for his wrath today. We have a trial for the end-of-term exams and I want to be on my game. My grades slumped in years 5 and 6 due to being bullied, this won't be happening in high school.

"That arsehole needs to be put in his place." It's Nigel, one of the geeks in our group. He had watched what happened and has fallen in behind me.

"Yep. Are you coming to the park this afternoon?" I whisper not wanting others to hear.

"Wouldn't miss it. Can't wait to hear what you and Trudi have planned."

I don't answer as we don't really have a plan. *Yet.* Scenarios are going through my mind all the time, but mostly they involve me being Milly. We can't rely on me transforming all the time. *Oh, how I wish I was able to control this. Hey, Sis, help out here, please.*

Buster walks past us and punches both our arms with an evil smirk. He glares back at us and gives us the finger.

"Wanker," blurts Nigel loud enough for Buster to hear. I laugh nervously even though I'm trying to stay calm. Luckily, Buster keeps moving away from us.

After school, we're all at the park. It's close to Trudi's house so most of us can walk home from here. The park is deserted, which is good for us as we don't want anyone hearing what we're discussing. We are seventeen including Trudi and me. I'm pleased to see everyone has turned up for our first meeting since high school began.

I wait as everyone stops murmuring and turns towards me to listen. "You've all done well with sending us ideas, Trudi is impressed with some of the ones the girls have sent. Especially you, Athena, you're channelling those evil brutes, obviously."

Athena laughs, "I'm not ready to be bullied throughout high school, we need to fight fire with fire." She looks around from her position at the front as everyone nods. Nigel is next to her giving her a smile.

"Ok, I'll make this quick as we should all be home studying. Right, we keep doing what we have been, keeping an eye out for bullies doing their deeds and pouncing on them." Trudi snickers next to me and I realise I've referenced Milly without knowing. She is still the only one who knows I transform and we're keeping it that way.

She takes over. "I've collated all your ideas and sent everyone a spreadsheet. They are in order of suitability. Nigel, your idea of putting them up naked against a wall and interrogating them with the threat of posting on socials – I laughed at this one, but it's not plausible is it?"

"They go too far so I thought we could too." Everyone laughs.

"It's last on the list, Nige, but who knows, if Buster becomes a super pain, we'll think about it." This brings more laughter from the group.

"Ok, thanks Trudi. Now let's all get home and look at

those ideas after we finish studying. We'll implement probably the top three and go from there. Sound good?" There are shouts of 'yeah' and 'great' as everyone disperses and heads home.

NINE

Trudi

Magic and Werecats

I'm back home and picking up my clothes off the floor. My parents are downstairs vacuuming and mopping. This household is routine-driven, which suits my OCD personality, but it doesn't mean I enjoy cleaning. In fact, I hate it and hope to one day be able to afford someone to do it for me. Damn it, I should be studying right now not wasting my time cleaning.

As I continue tidying I think about Edward and his secret, how incredible it is. And he chose me to share it with! I am honoured and I need him to know I will keep his secret because of how I feel about him sharing it with only me. We have become good friends, which for people like us isn't easy. I am tall like Edward, wear glasses, the skin on my face has red, infected pustules and cysts the size of currants. Some turn purple after I'm done with them, which looks even more gross. Anyway, back to Edward's secret – there were rumours surrounding Milly and her powers when I met her in kindergarten, but most kids scoffed saying it was all a myth. Well, Edward has proved to me that it's more than a myth. Incredibly, it's true.

Milly took her secret to her grave, and to tell you the truth, I don't remember her disappearing as much as Edward does. She was obviously able to control the transforming, whereas Edward doesn't know how. I wonder whether he'll learn how as he becomes better acquainted with this magic. Hmm, I might do some research about this type of magic and see if I can help him somehow.

With the tidying completed, I sit to do some study. A few hours later I hear my mother calling from downstairs, "Trudi, come and help with dinner. Set the table please."

"Oof, another chore," I mutter as I close my laptop.

It's Monday already and I'm moaning to Edward that weekends disappear too fast. He laughs but has his nose in his phone. "Hey, I looked up the word therianthropic, the magical ability of humans to metamorphose into animals." Immediately Edward looks up from his phone, "And?"

"It's also known as Shape Shifting. And you and Milly, when transformed, are known as Werecats. You both shape shift into a domestic cat, in your cases, a ginger. There is a lot of folklore around Werecats, especially in Europe in the early 1900s."

"Ok, this is all very interesting, but why did you look this up?" I didn't go into the fact I already know what shape shifting is, it's what I do…occasionally.

"Aren't you curious why you can't control when you transform? I was researching to see if I could help you with this."

Edward stops and his face changes, "I have thought about me being able to control how and when it happens but haven't look into it yet. That would be cool. Maybe I can't control it because this magic has been handed down from my sister?"

"Possibly," I reply taking in his new-found interest. "Unfortunately, I couldn't find anything about controlling the magic."

"Na, thanks anyway. I might do some of my own research and see what I can find out. There must be others who have these powers."

I nod as the school bell rings indicating we need to go to assembly. Well, it looks like I have helped Edward to a point, he might find out more about his magic now. Imagine how powerful this will be in sorting out the bullies if Edward can get the timing of his transformations right.

TEN

Jackson

    The Nice One

I'm sitting at my desk in my room, studying. Buster was being a real pain in the arse today, I don't know why I bother with him. He was merciless with three of the Year 7 kids, one of whom cried and went to sick bay asking for his mother. I felt physically sick when I heard that had happened. Buster doesn't seem to know when to stop.

Thinking I should speak to one of the girls about this, maybe Isla, she's the more sensible of the two, I wonder whether she is trustworthy enough not to blurt this to Buster or her cousin, Willow. I sit with this thought for a minute but…probably not. I discard the idea for now.

Closing my laptop, I head towards the kitchen to find my mother preparing dinner. "Hi, sweetheart, you hungry?" Mum is always preparing food with four men in the house, luckily for us she can cook. "Yeah, I could eat. Do you need any help?"

"Please. See those potatoes, peel them, thanks."

I take the potatoes to the other side of the bench and begin peeling them.

Mum asks, "You seem to have settled in well at this school. I hope we won't be moving again, with you in high school now, I've asked your father to stay put this time."

Those words are gold, this is what I've wanted for years, to stay at one school long enough to make true, long-lasting friendships. I don't see Buster as being a long-term friend, but if we stay here, I won't need him to be. I'm sure I can make other friends and leave Buster and his *gang* to their petty bullying. "Do you think Dad will stay at this job, Mum?"

"I hope so, he's going for a promotion so he won't have to leave to go to a better job. Like you boys, I'm tired of moving house."

I smile and keep peeling the potatoes. This is the first time either of my parents has discussed this with one of us. We boys were never given the opportunity to decide where or when we moved. In fact, we were usually told at the last minute. This is my fifth school since starting kindergarten, and if mum is right, I will finish my school life at Redman High.

I'm walking behind Buster when he begins tormenting a young girl. We're in Year 10 and this poor little Year 7 kid is frightened by this bully asking for her lunch money. "Buster, give it a rest. Really? You're attacking girls now."

"Shut the fuck up, Jon. I do what I bloody well like. You're not the boss of me."

He always gets my name wrong. "It's Jackson, and no, I won't shut up. Enough already, it's Friday morning and you've hassled too many kids this week." As I'm talking the girl runs off while Buster is distracted.

"Now look what ya did. She's gone and I don't have any money for a snack later today."

"That's your problem," I say as I walk towards the lockers.

Isla, who was standing behind me with Willow, follows

me and says, "Wow Jack, you stood up to Buster. That's brave." Willow calls out to her but she waves her goodbye, "I'll catch up, you go."

"He's pissing me off. Honestly, he's bothering girls now, what the hell is he thinking?"

Isla puts her head down, "Yeah, that's a bit crap. But as he said, Buster does what he wants."

"Yeah, but this is too far. Why do you stick around? You're not his girlfriend."

"I do whatever Willow does, she's my cousin and we've always done things together. I don't like what Buster does either, but it makes us look cool and other kids look up to us."

"In front of you maybe, but behind your backs, I'm not so sure. Besides, there are other popular girls you could hang out with."

"You're right. I'll make a point of sitting with them at lunch and see if Willow follows me. If she does, then Buster can go and get stuffed."

That was surprisingly easy, I didn't think Isla would leave her comfort zone. I'm sure hanging around with Buster has its benefits, at least they are protected by him. I guess that's the reason I stick around too, he protects me as well. But because of what he just did, I'm wondering whether it's worth me sticking around. Maybe I'll take Isla's tack and sit with others at lunchtime. It's time I found some new friends that are more my style.

Later that afternoon, we're waiting outside the fish shop for Buster to get his order. I'm eating my hot chips and the hot, salty oil is making my fingers red raw. But I like to eat my chips hot, I hate them cold and rubbery.

I hear a commotion and see Buster holding up a kid by the scruff of the neck. "You little shit, you knocked over my chips." He is screaming and then, to everyone's horror, he pushes the poor kid, who is half Buster's size, down to the ground. "Eat them," his voice booms and heads turn. I walk over, "Buster, stop," I say helping the boy up who is crying and blabbering that he's sorry.

"Fuck off, Jon, or Jack, whatever your bloody name is. This isn't your fight. This kid knocks over my food and you're helping him? What the fuck?" With this he knocks the boy down again and rubs his face into the fallen chips. I hear a crack.

"Stop, you're hurting him." The boy sits up and places his hands on his nose. I hear him faintly say it's broken. "Shit, Buster, this is abuse. You've broken his nose, I'm calling Triple 0, he needs medical help."

"Ah, fuck this. You be the nice one then, I'm off home. This isn't my fault." I grab his arm and he turns, his eyes black with scorn, "Take your hand off my arm before I do somethin' you'll regret." He whispers this menacingly and I drop his arm with force. I need to help this injured kid, it doesn't matter that Buster is leaving, I'll inform the medical team what happened here.

The paramedics arrive within ten minutes and I tell them the whole story, who Buster is and how he does this almost like a hobby. "Nice kid," says the female paramedic sarcastically, "bullies think they're invincible. Anyway, well done for helping, Jackson, we'll take it from here."

I thank them and begin heading home. This is the last time I'm going to have anything to do with Buster. I refuse to be part of his gang any longer. If he can be this senseless by abusing and physically hurting kids then he needs to be taught a lesson.

ELEVEN

Edward
The New Member

I'm sitting at the park bench waiting for the other geeks to arrive. We've become a cohesive group and are all good friends. And we're making progress with managing the bullies. Until Buster did the unthinkable. He's been suspended for a month because he broke a boy's nose, Jackson let the paramedics know and the school principal was alerted. Buster wasn't even a bit remorseful, in my opinion he deserves further punishment.

The sun is beaming down and the bench is warm even though it's autumn. As I scroll through my phone looking for others who may have my power a message comes through from Trudi, she's on her way. I'm still scrolling when I am startled by a tap on my shoulder.

"Hi, sorry, I didn't mean to scare you."

I look up to see Jackson and can't keep the surprise from my face. "Umm, hi…"

"I wanted to apologise to you and your friends. Buster is a menace, I want to help you guys because I'm embarrassed at being part of his gang." Obviously, Jackson is worried about the look on my face as he continues with, "I'm being honest, this is not a joke and I'm not trying to trick you in some way."

"Err, sorry, this is such a surprise. Weren't you tormenting us geeks last month?"

"Guilty, but since the kid was hurt I've decided to make better friendships. I'm here to help you guys, I know how Buster thinks. And I'm his age, I can stand up to him with you all as backup. What do you think?"

I'm gobsmacked and eventually ask him to sit down as others begin to stroll towards us. The looks on their faces are as confused as mine was when Jackson tapped my shoulder. "It's alright, Jackson is on our side now."

"Really? Wow." This from Nigel with others also commenting and acknowledging Jackson with nods and handshakes. Anthea and Trudi walk up together having heard and also greet Jackson. There is general chatter as we wait for a few more people then Trudi starts proceedings.

"Welcome everyone and thanks for your time yet again. Since our last meeting, you all voted and I'd now like to announce the top three strategies we're going to work with."

1. Intervene when you see bullying…but safely. Have your phone ready to video. Show the recording to the bully and threaten to post it.
2. Let's pick a teacher we can trust, maybe Mr Ferris? We let him know what we are doing.
3. If someone is physically hurt, call triple zero and inform the police. This is assault.

There is a round of applause as I take over. "Thanks Trudi and I think you'll all agree they are good strategies. Well done voting everyone." I continue asking everyone to keep vigilant and we all agree that Trudi and I are to speak with Mr Ferris. Then, I discuss Jackson being here and allow him to speak.

"Well, I saw the shock on your faces when you all arrived and they were justified. As I explained to Edward, after Buster hurt that Year 7 boy I was disgusted and decided to change my life. I hope you will trust that I will help you to beat these bullies, I'm on your side. Using my knowledge of how bullies think, especially Buster, I will be an asset, I promise."

Cheers break out, applause and whistles also fill the park. Trudi and I smile at each other.

I stand up next to Jackson and offer my hand, "Welcome to the geeks club, Jackson. We're sure you will be an asset to our cause. Now, after this successful meeting, let's head home and I look forward to seeing you all at school next week. Enjoy your weekend everyone." We start dispersing with Trudi, Jackson and myself heading out of the park in the same direction.

We're silent until Trudi breaks it by asking a question as we arrive at her house, "So glad you're onboard, Jackson, what made you be part of the bullies' group anyway?"

"It's a long story, but I was lonely. This is my fifth school since starting school and I met Buster in the school holidays at a soccer trial. I was just happy to have made a friend before starting at yet another new school."

Trudi nods, "I can't imagine you being lonely with two brothers, but I guess you need your own friends, right?"

I realise Trudi has just divulged she knows more about Jackson than he has told us yet. If he's annoyed, he doesn't show it.

"Definitely, my brothers are ok but annoying at the same time. Being the eldest means they look up to me, which can be overwhelming. They're also pranksters making them even more annoying."

"I get that, although I miss Milly so much now. We had our moments when our sibling rivalry became intense, but I'd do anything to have that back." I say this without thinking and then regret bringing the mood down. "Sorry, I blurted that out didn't I?"

"You have every right to, mate. I shouldn't have ranted about my brothers, I can't imagine what you're going through." Jackson nudges my shoulder, I think we're going to get on. "Gotta go, see you both on Monday."

"Bye." Both Trudi and I say this in unison. When he's out of earshot, I say, "Well, that's a turn up, a bloody good one."

"Yep, he's going to be a bonus. I always wondered what he was doing in that gang, he seemed too nice."

"Yeah, you've mentioned that before. See ya Monday, Trudi," I say walking towards my place with a huge smile on my face.

The next morning I find myself in the kitchen as Milly the cat, which is a surprising because I'm not angry nor have I been bullied this past week. Mum is making coffee and I meow. She doesn't notice, which is when I realise I have transformed as invisible Milly. Cool.

I brush myself against Mum's leg to see if she reacts. She looks down and rubs her leg but doesn't say anything. Wow, she can feel me but can't see me, or hear me either. Ok, time to put this situation to good use. I decide to visit Jackson's house to ease my mind that he's not conning us. Last night my mind kept going over his offer of helping us with some negative thoughts niggling at me. A visit will banish these thoughts, I hope.

As I walk outside through my front door, being invisible allows me to go through inanimate objects, I smell rain. It's only light and doesn't bother me and soon I'm out the front of Jackson's house. I slip in through his front door the same as I did with my own. I find him at the kitchen bench eating breakfast, he's watching something on his phone and laughing. I can hear laughter coming from his phone too and realise he's watching a comedian we all know, a popular Aussie one.

"What's so funny?" One of his brothers has walked in.

Jackson is still laughing, "This guy is hilarious." He shows his phone to his brother.

"Yeah, I guess so. He's a bit of a bogan."

"What would you know." Jackson scoffs and turns his attention back to his phone.

"Mum was wondering why you arrived home late after school yesterday."

"I explained why, went to see some friends at the park. None of your business, really."

"I wasn't worried, Mum was. Didn't know you had friends."

"Toby, you're such a shithead. Yes, I have friends, Edward and Trudi if you must know."

"Those geeks, they're in my year. What the fuck are you doing hangin' with them?"

"Again, none of your business who I choose to hang out with. Now, piss off will you."

"Just making convo, big bro, chill out." Toby leaves stewing with anger.

So this is what Jackson was talking about yesterday, how his siblings can be annoying. I get it but decide to get on with why I'm here.

His bare feet are dangling on the stool and I rub myself against them. He flinches and bends down to rub his toes. Suddenly, I'm no longer invisible. What the…?

He sees me before I can escape. "What the hell, what are you doing in my house? And how did you get in?" He jumps off the stool and places his hand near my nose. I allow him to scratch my head. "You're a cute ginger, aren't you. You had better go, my little brother is allergic to cats, come on, out you go." He directs me out the door.

I stand on the stoop staring at his front door as he closes it. He is actually nice and seems to like cats, I'll let him be part of our group.

TWELVE

Edward and Buster

I've lined up at the canteen and am starving, my stomach is doing backflips. Running late for school this morning, I skipped breakfast. Minding my own business I turn to see Buster is behind me. Thought I could smell that hint of body odour combined with a waft of self-assurance. He's stoned, as usual.

"My mate, Eddie. Did I see you with Jackson this morning? Since when are you friends?"

"Just being friendly." I keep my interaction with him short.

"What makes you think you can be friends with him? He's my mate and is part of my gang. Fuck off and leave him alone."

I turn towards him and nod, "Ok."

"Good. Now let me in."

I do as I'm told and can feel my anger searing through my body. I breathe deeply to calm myself, all I want is to buy my lunch in peace. When I finally reach the counter, order and start walking to where Trudi is sitting, Buster is waiting for me.

He walks past sneering at us, "The geek and his girlfriend." He holds his finger up at us. We let him pass and out of sight before speaking.

"He's a bloody child." I say this with tension in my voice. "He told me I can't talk to Jackson, can you believe that?"

"Calm down, Edward. He's a jerk, don't let him get to you."

I know what Trudi means but it's hard to do when he pushes my buttons so easily. "If Jackson wants to be my friend, what has that got to do with Buster?"

"Are you seriously asking me *that* question?" Trudi looks at me like I have two heads. "Buster has a bullying gang and as far as he's concerned Jackson is part of it." She's right of course, but he still has no right to tell me, or Jackson, who to be friends with. I change the subject to whether anyone has noticed any bullying today, apart from my short interaction just now.

"No, not that I've heard. I still think we should let Mr Ferris know what we're doing, what about this afternoon after school?"

"Ok, meet you outside the teacher's staff room and catch him then." She nods and then stands to head to class. I sit for a bit longer allowing my fuming thoughts to dissipate, I have to learn to not let Buster annoy me.

Trudi is waiting outside the staff room when I turn up. "Is he in there?"

"Not yet, but he has to come here to get his bag before leaving. Let's wait."

"What are you two shits doing here? Detention for the good kids." Buster's maniacal laugh makes my skin crawl. Trudi places her hand on my arm making sure I keep quiet. The next minute, I'm Milly.

"What the fuck!" Buster's eyes are wide and I can't help

snickering. The funny thing is it comes out as a low, menacing meow. "Where the hell did the cat come from and where the hell is Eddie?" He looks around, twisting his body, bending down and then facing Trudi with a dumb look on his face.

I can see she is stifling a laugh, "What are you talking about, Buster, Edward was never here."

"Don't shit me, Trudi, he was…here." He points to where human Edward had been standing and as Milly, I jump up and bite his finger. "Ow, you mangy cat. Shit that stings." He looks at his finger and is about to suck it but thinks better of it.

I stand there sneering at him and Trudi picks me up as Buster is about to kick me. "Hey, don't hurt the cat, it probably thought you were going to do something bad pointing at it like that. That is an aggressive move to a cat."

"Oh, bullshit. It bit my finger for no reason."

"What's going on here and where did that cat come from?" It's Mr Ferris.

"I'm taking it home, Mr Ferris, it must have wandered away from its home." Trudi pats my head ensuring I stay calm. I squirm in her arms as I need to transform back to being me, we need to talk to Mr Ferris.

"Well, both of you had better be getting home. And this is the second time I've seen you hanging around school after the home bell, now off you go."

"Err, Mr Ferris, may I speak with you, I have something important to tell you." As Trudi says this I jump out of her arms because I want to transform so I can be with her when she does. And I don't want Mr Ferris to witness this. "Hey, Edw…umm, the cat, I need to go and find it."

"Yes, as I said both of you need to go. We can talk another time, Trudi." Mr Ferris walks past me, I'm still Milly. "And take this cat with you." I'm around the corner after he walks past and I make sure Buster and Mr Ferris are gone before I rub against Trudi's legs.

"Well, you stuffed that up, Edward. Come one, let's go home." I walk beside her as Milly until we're halfway home, then I'm Edward again.

"Oh, welcome back. Bit late though."

"Sorry, I still have no control when it happens. And the day I went to Jackson's house, I hadn't been bullied all week. The only thing I can put it down to is I was worried that he was lying to us about helping out."

Trudi stops and looks at me, "Seriously, why would he do that? What secrets do we have that he would share with other bullies?"

I feel stupid having told her my thinking but try not to show it. Trudi and the other girls aren't bullied as much as us boys, so I don't argue. "Yeah, you're probably right. I was worried about nothing." When and how I transform is becoming more confusing each time.

The following day I snicker when I see Buster at school with a fat bandage on his middle finger getting sympathy from Willow and Isla.

After school, Trudi and I are happily talking about our chat with Mr Ferris as we head home. At first he said he didn't believe in magic but had heard the rumours about Milly. "There have been many unexplained events, not just those surrounding your twin, I'll give you that," he had said. Eventually, he came round to believing me, especially with Trudi backing me up. He agreed to help us and gave me his assurance he would not divulge the secret.

THIRTEEN

Edward
  Mr Ferris Champions Our Cause

Buster is chasing me and I see the science lab door is slightly ajar. Two days ago, he had bullied me by taking my lunch (yet again) and teasing me about Trudi being my girlfriend. This afternoon I transformed into Milly just as the school bell rang. Buster was the first to see me and bolted towards me as I ran into the lab. I peed in a few places, this happens when I'm agitated.

I can hear Willow and Isla whispering outside the door as Buster leers at me. "Come here, let me show you the scars I have due to you scratching me. You need to pay for what you're doing to us."

In a flash, I'm back to being Edward and Buster does a double take, "What the fuck, where did the cat go?"

I laugh, "What cat? It's just you and me in here. Haven't you had enough today, Buster? Can we call a truce?

"Not until you tell me what the hell happens, one minute

there's a ginger cat roaming around, then you're here denying a cat was ever here."

"You're delusional, that cat is safely at home with his owner. This owner makes sure it doesn't roam."

"Oh really!" His voice rises a few octaves. "How are you so sure?"

"Because I was the one who took the cat to his new home, it's a very secure house, the old brick place down the end of my street."

"The one where the old hag lives? How the hell can she look after a cat."

"What's it to you? She's happy to have her."

"Shit, enough of this. That cat was just here, I swear. Can't you smell the cat pee?" I remain quiet wanting to get out of this room and go home. "Stuff this, get the fuck out of my face, Eddie, I've had enough of you today." I gladly leave but not before I see him pulling at the burner cords.

The meeting at the park, the second one for this month, has everyone talking about the Bunsen Burner incident. Like Mr Ferris, no one can believe Buster's stupidity.

"Alright, it's time we started." I wait until everyone settles before continuing, "Now, Mr Ferris wants us to rein in what we do to intimidate the bullies. In other words, we help by stopping the bullying and taking victims being bullied away to safety. Then, that's it. Don't interact with the bullies making them angrier and putting yourselves in danger." I look around as everyone nods.

Nigel pipes up, "What if they don't let it go and have a go at us, do we just take their shit?"

Trudi speaks before I can answer, "Good point, Nigel, but it's still best to leave it and help the kid in need. Take them to their home or to a safe place and let the bullies stew. Better that than you guys getting hurt."

Jackson is next to speak, "This is the way to deal with bullies, if you don't react, they will calm down eventually.

The object is to keep bullied kids safe, not to intimidate the bullies. Mr Ferris, who by the way, is on our side, is right to ask us to stay safe as well."

"Yeah, it was a good idea having a teacher involved. Mr Ferris is a good choice," says Nigel.

Everyone starts to disperse and heads home while Trudi, Jackson and I sit on the park bench discussing what has happened since Jackson joined our group. Things have improved a little with less year 7 kids being bullied, especially when Jackson is around. He prides himself in just having to turn up for the bullies to stop, rarely does he have to say anything. This is a big plus for us and with the Jackson and Milly combination, we're winning the fight against the bullies.

The next day we are in Mr Ferris' office because of the science lab incident. In attendance are Trudi and I along with Buster, Willow and Isla.

There is silence while Mr Ferris seems to be thinking about what he will say. Then, "You are the most irresponsible student I have ever had." This is directed at Buster. "But Sir…"

"Don't interrupt me when I'm talking. Do you know the danger you placed my students in by tampering with the electric Bunsen Burners? What the hell were you thinking?"

"It wasn't me, it was that stupid cat." We all snicker under our breath. "What? it's true."

Mr Ferris scoffs, "Wow, that's even better than 'the dog ate my homework'." We all crack up laughing, Mr Ferris included. Although he quickly stops when he realises he's the adult in the room. Given he's only ten years older than Buster, his sense of humour is still intact with only a few years' teaching under his belt. "You are suspended for a week." Buster is about to protest but thinks better of it when Mr Ferris raises his hand.

"Now, Willow and Isla, you both told me you had nothing

to do with this other than stand outside the door making sure no one saw what was happening. They both nod and Willow speaks, "We saw Buster running after the cat who had entered the semi-opened door in a rush of fur and mewing. The cat seemed angry and agitated."

"And that's when he spat and peed on the cord of the burner on table one."

Mr Ferris keeps a straight face with difficulty, "You think this caused the electric burners to become faulty?"

Buster looks around unsure whether to answer, so he simply nods.

"This was the afternoon before the failure, surely the urine would have dried by then," Mr Ferris keeps interrogating Buster.

"Yeah, probably. But by that time the corrasion had started." We snicker again at Buster's apparent disregard for the English language, he has no idea.

"Buster, you have it wrong. Cat urine corrodes stainless steel, not plastic cords. Now, what did you do to the burners."

"I swear, Sir, nothin'. It was that mangy cat. Maybe it chewed the cord before peeing on it."

Mr Ferris lets out a frustrated breath, "Buster, go home. We'll see you next week. Stay home and out of trouble, I'll be checking in with your parents. Girls, make sure he goes straight home."

Trudi and I are left standing waiting to speak with Mr Ferris. He starts talking when he's sure Buster and the girls are gone. "Edward, are you absolutely sure you saw Buster fiddle with the cords?"

"As I was leaving, he was pulling at one of them, Sir."

"I can't get my head around why he would do something so stupid. You've told me he was mad at you not believing him about the cat, but is this enough to place everyone at risk? We could have had a serious fire."

"He has a short fuse," I chuckle.

"Edward, this is serious. I do appreciate you and your friends including me in on what you do to help the kids being bullied, and Milly the Cat seems to get away with a lot, but let's not allow things to go too far. Intimidating bullies to the point where their anger makes them reckless is not acceptable."

"Sorry, Sir. And we appreciate you supporting us and keeping my secret, but the likes of Buster don't seem to learn, they keep bullying. Yesterday and the day before, he was relentless with me and others, maybe that's why he was so angry."

"Yes, that's unfortunate but there is not much I am able to do without outing you as Milly."

Trudi speaks for the first time, "No, we certainly don't want this secret going any further. We'll talk with the others and see how we can intimidate without antagonising the bullies."

"Ok, I'll leave you to it. You had better go home now, see you both tomorrow."

"Thanks, Mr Ferris, we all appreciate your help." He gives us a knowing smile as we all walk out of the science lab.

FOURTEEN

Edward
Milly Disappears

Something strange has happened. I haven't transformed into Milly since the Bunsen Burner incident, even if I've been bullied, which thankfully is less now. Maybe this is why Milly isn't helping out, she thinks we're handling this well enough. *Is that right, Milly? Are we making enough of a dent that I don't need to transform?"* I wait almost expecting an answer even though that's not possible.

Looking back at my computer screen, I'm struggling to finish my assignments. Deciding to leave it, I head towards the kitchen and find mum preparing dinner.

"Hi darling, are you hungry?"

That is a stupid question to ask a twelve-year-old boy who is always hungry. "Sure am, what's for dinner anyway?"

"Your favourite, Shepherd's Pie. Set the table, it's almost ready."

It's funny she says to set the table, with only two of us now, it takes seconds. As I clatter about in the cutlery drawer,

I mention that Milly hasn't been around for the past two months.

"Really?" she answers placing the piping hot pie onto the table. The delicious smell fuels my hunger even more. "Any idea why, or is this a good thing?"

"Yeah, Buster hasn't bothered me as much and with the help of our group, he rarely gets away with much now. Maybe Milly thinks we can handle things ourselves from now on?"

Mum scoops out a healthy serving of the pie onto my plate and pushes the salad over to me in the hope I might eat some greens. That's unlikely, me and green food don't mix.

"Well, that's good news. It's about time Buster was put in his place. Do you miss being Milly?"

I think about this as I stuff pie into my mouth breathing in to cool it. "Oh, that's hot," I say with my mouth still full, which brings on a look from mum. She is a stickler for manners, especially at the dinner table. "I miss Milly every day, but funnily enough I only noticed a few days ago that I hadn't transformed since that day. I guess not needing to fight bullies means she is leaving me to it."

Mum wipes a tear from her eye, talking about my twin is still raw and I know she misses Milly as much as I do. "I wouldn't worry about this too much, she'll come back when she's ready, especially if you need her to. Hopefully only in emergencies because the bullies are finally beginning to see reason."

With yet another mouthful, I nod and we remain quiet for the rest of dinner.

Trudi and I are walking home with Nigel and Athena. We're discussing how things have been quiet on the bullying front and that we haven't seen the ginger cat around.

"I wonder what's happened to that cat. It turned up every time we needed it, have any of you seen it?"

Trudi answers Athena, "Nuh, I did notice that it hasn't been around though. Edward?"

"The lady down my street is looking after it, as far as I know things are ok, they are both happy with each other's company. Besides, with the bullying not so frequent now, there's no need for it to be around." I say this with the most non-committal voice I can muster.

"What intrigues me," says Nigel, "is how it knew to be around at the right time? It's almost like it has superpowers, I don't know… maybe some instinctive vision of good against evil." We all laugh.

"That's cool, imagine being able to know when something bad is going to happen and you're able to stop it. But I guess that's what superheroes do." Trudi is still laughing as she says this.

We arrive at Nigel's and Athena's street and say our goodbyes. Our friendship has grown this year, we spend a lot of our free time with them.

"Those two are good value, maybe we can let them in on the secret?"

I look at Trudi and say, "Hmm, maybe one day, but not yet. I think enough people know about my magic for now, and anyway, has it disappeared? Who knows when I will transform again?"

"I guess so, but I can't imagine you've lost it altogether. How have you gone with finding others with these powers?"

I explain how my research was sketchy at first, but I have now found a society that meets once a month. "The A-Alliance is a group of people with all sorts of magical powers, some better than others. I'm going to my first meeting next Friday. But now that I'm not transforming, I'm wondering whether I should go."

Trudi stops, turns to me and holds my shoulders, "That's great news and you must go." She's looking directly into my eyes and I turn away, I'm uncomfortable looking people in the eye, even someone like Trudi who I know well. "You need to meet people who are like you and learn from them. Maybe this is why Milly is leaving you alone, she wants you to find out more about your power."

Trudi is right. I shrug away from her staring, yet caring, eyes. "Ok, I'll go on Friday."

"Great, where are you meeting?"

"Sorry, Trudi, that's top secret."

"Ha, of course, that was a stupid question. See you at school on Monday," she says as she heads towards her street. I stand out the front of my place for a bit longer watching my best friend walk away, I'm glad she is the one I trusted with my secret. Between her and Mr Ferris, and Mum, of course, my secret is safe.

FIFTEEN

The A-Alliance

I stand out the front of a derelict house wondering whether it's safe to go in. It's near the old quarry, an area no one frequents other than drug addicts and feral cats. I caught two buses to arrive. I had texted Mum and let her know I'd be late home, told her I was at Jackson's house studying.

Someone drives up and parks their car in the driveway. She steps out and walks towards me. "Hi, I'm Ester, welcome. You must be new. Most new members have that look on their face when they see my house." She places her hand out and I shake it.

I take in her stocky figure, grey-tinged hair and pleasant smile. "Yeah, hello, it doesn't look safe. I'm Edward Shipley."

"The façade is deceiving, we're a secret alliance as you will soon find out. The website you went on is just a landing page for new members. Come on let's go inside, you'll see a very different house."

"Wow." This escapes my mouth before I can stop it. The amount of people here, they can't possibly all be magicals.

Which is a stupid thought otherwise they wouldn't know about this place. I'm still in awe as I walk further as I have walked into a magical wonderland of bright sunshine with Jacaranda trees in full bloom – some growing inside, others out, along with a meadow towards the horizon full of bees, bright flowers and butterflies. There are also animals – dogs, cats, horses, birds, all in various states of slumber. I want to ask so many questions, especially how they stop rain coming into the house where the trees are growing inside? The Jacarandas growing indoors jut out through the roof.

"Impressive isn't it?" Ester takes me out from my wonder.

"I… ah, don't know what to say."

She laughs and asks me to follow her towards the meadow where I can now see others mingling.

"Alliance members, meet Edward Shipley, our newest member."

I look around as people of all ages come up and say hello, shake my hand, and then return to where they were before. A few I notice are quite elderly, there are also people my age and younger. There must be hundreds of magicals here, I'm both amazed and proud. Who knew there were so many people who have powers like mine.

"Hello, I'm Sallyanne, the youngest member. Everyone calls me Sally. I knew your sister Milly." A girl walks up towards me as I take in her small stature, milky skin and blonde hair so light it's almost white.

"Oh, hello, nice to meet you." I can't keep the surprise out of my voice.

"Milly was a member with us for two years before… well, you know."

"I never knew that, but I guess I will learn about her being a member as well as my magic."

"We'll talk after the meeting, Ester, our chairperson will be starting soon." I follow her to where seats have been set up and she offers a seat next to hers. I am so intrigued with what will happen and can't wait to hear more about Milly from Sally.

Ester clears her throat, "Welcome alliance members and I call this meeting to order. For those of you who are new, we have this quarterly meeting to discuss issues with our magic, teach and guide those of you who may be floundering, and the best part – share each other's ideas and magical powers. I invite you all to stay after this meeting and mingle, get to know each other." She continues with an agenda of issues, talks about the good being done with their magic within the community, and then asks if anyone has questions. This causes a flourish of hands to go up and Ester patiently calls each person by name and listens to their questions. I learn so much within this first hour, my head is spinning.

Before I know it, the meeting is over and people leave their seats heading towards a table behind us laden with refreshments. *That wasn't there before?*

"Don't look so surprised," laughs Sally, this place is magical and things appear and disappear all the time."

"I didn't hear any noise behind us, that's what surprises me. They were so quiet."

"You'll find out about how things happen around here the more you come to these meetings. Ask questions and you'll learn faster." Sally asks me to follow her to the table and help myself to whatever I want. The choice seems endless – meats, pasta, vegetables, sweets and I see others piling their plates high. It all smells so delicious, so I can understand why. When we both have our plates full we walk to a bar table and begin eating while Sally talks about Milly.

"Like you, Milly came to us not knowing everything about her powers. Look at this alliance as an educational facility for people like us. She learned quickly and then helped other newcomers."

"Oh right, I thought Milly knew everything about her magic, I just assumed she did."

"Those of us born with our powers self-learn some of them, but there is always something else to learn. Ester will supply you with a pack to take home, keep it safe and don't let anyone see it, not even your mother. There is secret information contained within that pack that is only for magical people."

"Ok, noted. So, you and Milly were friends?"

"Yes, we helped each other with our magic. My power is that I can conjure things, good and bad. I'm eleven now and am mostly able to control whether I conjure up something good or bad. This is thanks to coming here for the past three years."

I'm amazed that a girl so young is allowed out till this late, it's already eight o'clock. "Don't your parents wonder where you are?"

"They're both magical and are standing over there." She points to two adults who are speaking to Ester. Her mother is an older version of Sally – blonde straight hair, tall and slim. She is dressed in an elegant pants suit and her husband, who is slightly shorter than her, is also in a suit. They are a handsome looking couple. "I could ask you the same question, you're not much older than me."

"I'm thirteen next month. I told my mother I'm at a friend's place. Although, if I don't leave soon, she will worry."

"Well, come with me, I'll introduce you to my parents and Ester will make sure you receive The Pack." I follow diligently having so many more questions I want to ask.

Sally's parents greet me warmly and Ester asks me to wait while she goes to the front of the house to get my pack. She's back within seconds much to my surprise. She obviously notices my face and explains, "I can speed up, commonly known as a 'speedster', but to the observer I seem to be walking at normal speed. This power confuses people, which is the whole point."

"I have so much to learn," I say taking The Pack from Ester. It's as light as a feather. "Is there anything in this?"

"Everything you will need. Now, let me see you out."

I say goodbye to Sally and her parents telling them I'll see them at the next meeting. They smile as I walk away with Ester, who is walking at normal speed this time.

SIXTEEN

The Pack

I'm at our front door and leave The Pack on the stoop not wanting my mother to see it and be curious. I needn't have worried, she was sound asleep on the lounge. She obviously had a big day because she is rarely asleep at this time of night. Returning to the open front door, I quickly bend down, pick up The Pack and run to my room.

"Is that you, Edward?"

"Yes Mum, be down in a minute." What I really want to do is open The Pack but I don't want to risk her coming into my room. I head downstairs leaving it under my bed. "Hi, sorry, I guess I missed dinner."

"No, I haven't eaten yet. Just flopped on the lounge after a big day… and well, yeah, I fell asleep. Want pizza?"

After all the food at the alliance house, I'm not hungry but I can always eat pizza. "Sure, I'll order."

"You're brilliant, thanks darling. I'm even too tired to think what I want. Buy the usual, please." I nod and bring up our local pizzeria on my phone.

In half an hour we're sitting on the lounge eating and talking about our theories as to why Milly has abandoned me. Mum's theory is that she's tired and needs to catch her breath. "She's been helping you for over a year now, she needs rest."

Is this even possible? Are you able to be tired when you're dead? "Maybe," I say hoping this is the end of the conversation as I want to be in my room discovering what is in The Pack. "I'm bushed, Mum and I need a shower. Thanks for the pizza." I stand up and take the boxes off the coffee table.

"I can't believe you left half of yours, are you not feeling well?"

"Nah, I'm fine. Jackson and I snacked on chips and stuff at his place. See you in the morning."

"Night, Edward, love you."

"Love you more," I reply as I head towards the kitchen. Leaving the pizza boxes near the recycling bin, which is full, I head to my room and shower as fast as I can. Honestly, I have the quickest shower I've ever had I'm that keen to see what is in store for me. I can't get back to my room quick enough.

Sitting on my bed I open The Pack.

Wow, I can't believe it. Ester was right, there is so much in there and I guess it's *everything I need* as she had told me when I was leaving. I'm about to dive in and discover…

"Edward, help!" Mum's scream is ear piercing as I run back downstairs.

I find her sitting on the floor clutching her arm. "What happened?" I ask telling her not to move as I get closer to her.

"Not sure, I fell asleep again and I must have been dreaming, because the next thing I'm on the floor. I fell on my wrist and it's awfully painful."

"Ok, stay put, I'm calling an ambulance. You're going to need that looked at." I feel sorry for Mum and hope the paramedics aren't too long. She's about to faint and I stop her just in time before she hits her head on the floor.

Once she is lying down and I know she's safe for now, I feel even more sorry for myself because I want to discover what's contained in The Pack. I guess that will have to wait until Mum is seen to.

Six hours later we're back home from emergency with Mum sporting a fresh cast up to her elbow. "I feel so stupid, I couldn't even explain how I fell. And sorry you've had to wait for me, Edward, you'd better get to bed."

"It's fine, Mum. As long as you're better. Besides, tomorrow is Saturday, I can sleep in."

"So it is, I forgot. Maybe I hit my head too. Still, it's after two, time we both went to bed."

"Goodnight, Mum."

"Goodnight, Edward. And I'm lucky you were home."

As I walk upstairs I realise things could have been a lot worse. With Mum being disoriented by the fall and feeling faint, she may have been on the floor for hours before she was found. She is lucky I was home. And The Pack? It will have to wait till later this morning as it's already early Saturday, it's three-thirty and I'm exhausted. Sleep comes easily as I crash onto my bed fully clothed.

SEVENTEEN

Buster

The Bullies Turn it up a Notch

I'm with Willow and Isla on the football field behind our school. Wiping my forehead, the sweat dripping off me. "It's bloody hot, how are you girls not sweating?"

"Yeah, well it is November so you're normal and girls don't sweat as much as boys," answers Willow. "Now, what's up, what are we doing here?"

I am about to answer when Isla interrupts, "We won't be long will we? I have things to do this afternoon."

"Give me a break. No, this won't take long. I've asked Nate and his crew to join us, we need reinforcements now Jackson has gone to the other side."

"What? You know I can't stand Nate, he's a big oaf with Artie not much better and why would I want him in our gang?" Willow is less than impressed as scorn covers her face. "Why do we need them all, we only lost one member?"

"If we join forces, Willow, we can stop the geeks from stopping us, especially now they have Mr Ferris on their side." I am about to keep talking when Nate arrives with Artie. "Hey, thanks for comin', where's the others?"

"It's just us until we know what this is all about," says Nate wiping his forehead, "and why the fuck are you guys in the sun? Let's get under the trees." We all follow Nate as he walks towards the creek and shade. "Now, you want our help?" he asks once we're all there.

"You know what's been happening, the geeks sometimes target your crew too. We need to stop this cause I need lunch money and I get my kicks seeing how scared those little twats get." Me and the boys snicker but the girls remain quiet.

"What's in it for us?"

"It's easy, the more of us, the more the power. And we can share what we get – money, food, whateva. We can't let those geeks get the better of us, I won't allow it."

"'suppose you're right. Let me put it to the girls and we'll come back to ya." Both Nate and Artie nod at each other.

"Cool, yeah, that's brill. Talk tomorrow, 'k?" I say as Nate puts out his hand and I grab it holding onto his wrist. "We'll be the best, I promise."

"Yeah, ok." Nate and Artie walk off with Artie giving Isla a long stare.

"Creep." Isla whispers this under her breath.

"They're both creeps," says Willow.

Two days later our gang is joined by Nate's crew and we go about being as brutal as before, in fact, worse.

"Hee, hee, you should have seen the look on the idiot's face when I pulled him down to my feet and made him lick my shoes. He gave me his money after that."

"That kid's parents are loaded, did you get a decent amount, Nate?"

"Twenty bucks, Buster, which ain't bad. He's going to be a target for a while now. What did you guys get up to today?"

"Willow here did well, had one of the geek girls in the loos screaming not to have her head put down the toilet because she'd just washed her hair the night before. Willow scored her lunch and ten bucks."

"Onya, Willow. And here I was thinkin' you didn't have the balls for this."

"Shut up, Nate, what would you know?" Willow sneers at him.

"Easy, I was givin' ya a compliment. Anyways, gotta go, me old man needs me to do errands." He clicks his fingers and Artie follows him along with Stella and Beth, their girlfriends. Both girls had stood back and gossiped totally ignoring the conversation.

"They're all such dicks," says Willow, "I still don't think this is a good idea, Buster."

"Why? We can help each other and share the spoils. I don't see what the problem is?"

"Making a kid lick his shoes, really? Come on, we're smarter than them."

"And threatening to put a girl's head down the toilet is smarter?"

"She annoyed me, so had it coming."

Isla pipes up, "You're all stupid. This bullying gig is stupid too, I've had enough."

We both look at Isla who starts walking away. "Oh, pardon me, you're too smart for us now," I call after her. She turns and gives me thc finger.

"She's been sitting with the popular girls lately, I thought something was up. Maybe she's going to do a runner like Jackson."

"Ah, fuck 'em both. With Nate and his crew, we don't need 'em. Hey, you coming to my place?"

Willow starts heading towards home, which is only a few streets away from school. "Na, got assignments to do. See ya tomorrow."

EIGHTEEN

The Geeks Revenge

The group is at the park and we have finished discussing the current spate of bullying. There are two weeks left before school breaks for the Christmas holidays with everyone keen to get them started.

I continue to address them, "… right, so we all agree Mr Ferris' involvement is a good thing. And we welcome Isla to our ranks, who along with Jackson, will help us to outwit the bullies." There is applause and loud whistles. "Now, a bit of housekeeping, this is our last meeting for this year and hopefully we'll get through the next two weeks without hassles. We'll meet again in February once school starts again. Have a great holiday and let us know if any bullies bother you during this time."

Athena speaks as I step down, "And a round of applause for Edward and Trudi for organising us like this. A job well done."

"Woo hoo." "Champions." "Thanks guys." Some come to thank Trudi and I personally, telling us how they are not so scared now they're part of this group. After most of them have dispersed and left the park, Jackson, Isla and Trudi are sitting on the bench looking up at me. "What?"

"You didn't discuss involving Isla before you introduced her to the group." Trudi is annoyed and isn't hiding it.

"That's because I thought of it on the spot. The bullies are more cunning now, doing things in secret and using lookouts. Stella and Bella keep an eye out for us geeks now."

"What can Isla do to help?" Trudi is standing with her hands on her hips, annoyance creeping all over her face not caring that Isla is there with them.

"As much as Jackson has, I know how bullies think too."

"Isla, you're new our side of things, but we have been dealing with bullies for a year now. By the way, you haven't told us why you decided to defect?"

She laughs, "Is that what I did? I guess I was fed up, they we using crueller tactics and I began feeling sorry for those poor kids. I was only in the gang because of Willow. I have other friends now, including you guys."

"Good for you," says Trudi. "Now, Edward, back to why you didn't involve us about Isla?"

"What the? I just told you it was off the top of my head. And everyone seemed to like the idea we have a new member. Besides, Jackson was introduced to the group straight away."

Trudi looks stumped. "Yeah, well, don't do that again. You and I need to discuss things before putting it to the group, it's safer that way."

Jackson laughs, "You two sound like a married couple. But maybe she has a point, Edward, you should discuss things with at least Trudi before blurting it out."

"Ok, I'll remember that. Now, who's for some hot chips?"

I'm in the science lab on the last Friday of school with Trudi, Jackson and Mr Ferris. He was surprised and shocked when we told him about my magic, having heard rumours, like most people he had dismissed them. He had looked at both Trudi and I asking whether this was a joke and I had replied, "The bullying is awful and has to be stopped, why would I like to an adult teacher about this?" Mr Ferris had contemplated this for a few minutes and said, "I will reserve judgement on your magic until I see proof of it, but anything we can do to reduce bullying is a good thing. Trudi and I hoped he would see reason, and a few days later when I transformed, the last time I was able to for a while, he was fully onboard. He also kept my secret to himself, I always knew he was trustworthy.

Since then, he has been great with helping us keep the bullies at bay. He organised the principal to address the whole school assembly on the virtues of being kind and accepting each other. Not that I think it was this that made them less likely to attack, but it may have helped. It was both Mr Ferris and us keeping an eye on anything untoward that has made the difference. We exacted our revenge.

"I commend you and your group on taking the initiative in stopping bullying, you are making a difference."

"Thanks Mr Ferris, your help was needed and has assisted us. After being bullied at primary school for two years, I was fed up. It feels good to be making a difference."

"You should, Edward. All of you should feel good about what you're doing. Next year we can keep things going and I'll take your lead on what you want me to contribute. Maybe we can look at an education program for the bullies teaching them how to behave and realise how bullying can have lifetime consequences."

Jackson nods, "That's what worried me, I didn't want to see someone in ten years' time still bearing the scars of what we did. So, thanks for taking me in, Edward and Trudi and I am looking forward to achieving more next year." Edward slaps Jackson on the back and smiles.

"Brilliant, then you're doing your job. Well said, Jackson.

Ok, time to get on home and start your holidays. Enjoy your break and see you back here at the end of January." We all shake Mr Ferris' hand and walk out into the sunshine. It's another hot and heavy December day, the humidity making our shirts sticky and stinky.

"See you soon, eh? Are you guys going away?" Jackson asks us.

Trudi simply shakes her head and I answer for both of us. "Nah, we're around. Maybe we can go to the beach or pool sometime?"

"Sounds good, let's keep in touch. Have a good Christmas."

"You too, Jackson," says Trudi smiling as we walk towards the gate and go our separate ways. "I'm proud of him." She says this when he's well out of earshot.

"Yeah, me too. You were right about him, he's too nice to be a bully. And it looks like Isla is nice as well."

"I'll reserve judgement on that until she proves herself. I did the same for Jackson."

"Ooh, you're tough sometimes, but I agree, she's only just come onboard." We head home in silence until we arrive at my place, wish each other a Merry Christmas and decide to make a date to go to the beach soon.

NINETEEN

Buster is Angry

The gang is all in my garage sitting amongst tools, car parts and rusted junk my stepdad collects. Nate, Artie, Stella and Beth have found places to sit semi-comfortably. I stand with Willow next to me. "They beat us down by keepin' a close watch and those bloody geeks 'ave got Mr Ferris now, he helps 'em."

"Yeah, and the principal too. That talk, it was all bullshit – we're supposed to love everyone and play nice. Holy shit is this utapia," drawls Artie, cigarette in his mouth.

"What the hell is utapia?"

"Geez, Buster, don't you know anythin'. It means a place that's perfect, everyone being happy, nice to each other and all that bullshit."

"Righ' ok. Listen, we need to be more cunning. I missed lunch for the last two weeks, me stepdad wouldn't give me any extra money. I'm a growing boy and he forgets how much I eat." The others nod agreeing with him. They continue discussing their plan of action for these holidays and for the next school year.

"We have to pick our times better," says Nate, "or try and distract Mr Ferris and the geeks before we pounce. Speaking of that, anyone seen the ginger cat around?"

"Not for a few months, maybe its dead. Good riddance." The girls whisper "aww" in unison. "What? That cat was a menace. One of the scratches it gave me festered and I was in emergency for hours. Had a technus shot and it bloody hurt."

"Fuck, I had one of those once, you're right, hurt like hell." Artie says this as he rubs his arm where the shot would have gone.

"Now, who's coming to the beach this weekend? I can ask me stepdad to take us in his truck unless you guys have transport." Willow shakes her head as do the other two girls and both Nate and Artie do the same. "Ok, I'll ask him at dinner before he gets too drunk."

They continue talking about their bullying plans and then discuss what they want to do for the new year. No one is going away because they don't have that kind of money so they're going to make their own fun at the beach and pools. Soon, I'm saying goodbye to them with Willow remaining behind.

I come back into the garage and grab her by the waist, "You staying over tonight?"

"Yeah, guess so. As long as your stepdad doesn't get too mad."

"Nah, he won't, he behaves himself when you're around." He kisses her with a sloppy kiss and whispers what he wants to do with her later.

Willow giggles kissing him back, then looks up at him, "What's with Artie's eyes? He's not Asian is he?"

"Somewhere way back in his family, yes. Chinese I think he said. His great-grandfather came to Australia from over there during the gold rush days."

"Right, they make him look at bit different. Part Aussie, part Asian."

"I guess so, never really thought about it. Artie is who he is. Now, where were we?" he sniggers.

The gang is at the beach, I'm sprawled on a double towel with Willow next to me posting on her phone. Nate, Artie, Stella and Beth are walking towards us.

"You wouldn't believe who's sitting over near the surf club? Edward along with some of his nerds. And Jackson."

"Well, well, that turd is here is he? Fuckin' left us for those nerds, thinks he's too good for us. Did he see you?"

"Yeah, we walked right past them. They all ignored us and 'the turd' as you call him, gave us the finger."

"Jerk, it's time I gave it to him, I've been quiet since he turned on us."

Willow puts her hand on his arm as he tries to get up, "Wait, don't do anything stupid here, Buster, the lifeguards are around. And all these people too."

Looking down at her after standing and shrugging her hand off me I say, "I don't give a shit about them, this is none of their business. You girls wait here, this won't take long." Willow begins to speak again but I just keep walking towards the surf club.

I see Edward stand as he sees the three of us heading towards them. "Right, you two get the other geeks, I'm concentratin' on the traitor." Nate and Artie nod.

"I ain't fighting the girls," says Artie.

"Sure, whatever. There's Edward and the other skinny one for you two."

I stand near the group flanked by Nate and Artie. Edward speaks first, "We don't want trouble, Buster. What do you want?" Nigel stands next to Edward as support.

"Just sayin' a friendly hello to youse. Nothin' wrong with that is there?" I know Edward doesn't believe me as I look over at Jackson. "How's it goin'? Haven't spoken in a while."

"Fine," Jackson spurts this out with disgust, "how about you guys go back to your girls, I'm sure they're missing you."

"I'll decide when I go back, you're not the boss of me. Just wanted to talk since, well you know, since you left."

"My decision, nothing to do with you."

"Coulda discussed things with me, didn't know you were upset. Did we do somethin' to upset ya?"

"Buster, I'm different now, ok. Leave it at that."

Nate and Artie make a move but I stop them. "Wait you two. And you don't have to be so rude, mate" I say making a move towards Jackson. Edward and Nigel move in front of me asking me to stand down.

"More of you tellin' me what to do. Fuck off you greasy weasels. I'm just talkin' to me old mate."

Jackson moves in front of Edward, "Buster, I'm telling you nicely, go back and enjoy the beach with your girls."

"Fuckin' hell, stop tellin' me what to do." My anger surges as I punch Jackson hitting his chin.

Trudi and Athena scream as Nate and Artie attack Edward and Nigel.

Edward transforms.

"What... where the hell did he go. And what's a cat doin' at the beach." Nate says looking around for Edward.

"Meowww," screeches Milly jumping up and scratching my legs as I try to kick her away.

"What the?" I watch on as Milly jumps on Nate and Artie scratching their arms.

"Ow, shit that stings," screams Nate who also tries to kick Milly but she is too quick.

"What the hell is going on here?" Two lifeguards approach the scene. "This beach is not a fight zone. We've called the police..."

I try to run but the lifeguards are too quick. Nate and Artie are still whining about their wounds.

"You're not going anywhere. All of you are to sit down

and wait for the police. This is disturbing the peace and assault. You, young man punched this boy without provocation, we saw you do this as we were headed this way. Now, sit down and behave."

The police arrive within minutes and take reports from witnesses while checking witnesses' phones as many of them had videoed the scene. Jackson, who had been taken by the lifeguards to treat the wound on his chin, turns to me whispering I will pay for this. I stare him down making sure he knows I'll be ready.

TWENTY

Edward
  Milly's Hologram

Trudi and the others stare as I look up at them as Milly. Other people on the beach stare too, it is unusual to see a cat on the beach, cats hate anything to do with water as we all know.

"Where's Edward?" asks Nigel.

"Don't know," says Trudi smirking looking down at Milly, "he seems to disappear whenever there is a fight."

"You're right, he does do that. I'll have to have a word with him, he can't be leaving us when we need him most."

"Good on you, but I'm sure there is an explanation for his disappearances."

"Oh really, Trudi? That will be interesting," says Athena, "I wouldn't pick Edward as being a coward."

As Trudi is about to answer, I sneak behind a sand dune and transform. Walking back towards them I say, "What's going on, why aren't you all relaxing on your towels?"

"Well, look who the cat dragged in," laughs Nigel. Trudi and I pass a knowing look between us trying not to laugh.

"Where the hell have you been? You missed a huge fight." Nigel continues explaining what Buster did and how the police took him away.

"Great, he's really in trouble this time."

"And where were you?" asks Nigel.

"I went to get a milkshake. I asked you all if you wanted anything, but you didn't answer."

"Where's the milkshake?"

"Nige, you know me, I drank it quickly. Man, it was good… thick and rich."

"So, you didn't see or hear anything?"

"I heard the police siren but didn't think it had anything to do with us. I guess we'll find out what happens to Buster online."

"Yeah, there are already posts about it," says Athena showing them her phone.

"Doesn't take long. I'll check mine later, right now I need a swim, it's bloody hot." I begin walking to the water's edge with Trudi following. As we reach the waves and allow them to gently soak our feet, I turn to her and smiles, "What's that look for?"

"Nothing, I'm amazed you transformed after so long."

"Me too. I guess I wanted to protect you all and it happened."

"Sounds likely," she says as she walks into the waves and dives in. I watch on and know she's not convinced but I'm not telling her about The Pack, that is my secret.

I've showered after our eventful day at the beach and am now in my room. Mum is out, which is convenient and it's the first time she's been out since hurting her wrist. One of her friends picked her up and they have gone to lunch. This means I have the house to myself for a few hours.

Opening The Pack, I conjure up Milly's hologram. "Hi Edward, how's my favourite brother?"

"I'm your only brother, Milly." She doesn't answer

because this hologram was produced before she died, but I love the fact I can see her and hear her voice again. I listen as she starts with lesson three of the metamorphosis series. I had a chance to listen to lessons one and two a few weeks ago, which came in handy at the beach earlier. Both these lessons helped me with controlling when I transform, it has a lot to do with controlling my breathing, summoning the cat hormones and using a mental chant to explain the place and time. This all worked perfectly at the beach, but there is so much more to learn.

Milly is showing me how to meditate when I'm near Jacaranda trees because this is where Milly was able to gather her strength to help her transform. "The purple flowers of this magnificent tree have magical powers that we can draw from, this is a great tool to use when you're feeling low, especially as transforming can sap your energy if you do it too often." *So that's the power of the Jacaranda. Makes sense as I have noticed gathering strength when I'm near one of them.*

As I listen, I look through the other gadgets, books and spells at my disposal in The Pack. I wonder whether I will ever need to use these, it is mainly the metamorphosis I'm keen on perfecting. When I'm at The A-Alliance next, I will ask Sally why I've been given all of these other resources that I may not need. I am looking forward to attending another meeting and speaking with the members, I am that keen to learn everything I can.

Jackson comes over the next day and Mum is surprised to see the damage to his face. He explains he slipped and fell at home, a stupid accident.

"Well, the shiner on your eye is quite scary, you must have given yourself a good old knock. Help yourselves to whatever is in the fridge, I'm off to work."

"Take care of yourself too, Mrs Shipley, Edward told me you hurt your wrist."

"Oh, yes, now that was a stupid accident. I fell off the

lounge," she laughs, "it's on the mend now, thanks for your concern." We watch on as she leaves us alone in the house. I do enjoy having the house to myself especially when Jackson or Trudi visit. He asks where she is and I explain she'll be here in an hour, had jobs to do at home first.

"Right then, let's go to my room. Want to play a game? My PlayStation is old and so are my games."

"Sure, I don't even own a game console, so you're one up on me."

"Really? With three boys in the house?"

"My parents don't believe video games are healthy and encourage us to work out or do something else that's productive." I don't answer as I open the door to my bedroom only now realising why on the few times I've been to Jackson's home, we had not played video games.

"Let me set this up and before we start I'll go down and get us some snacks. I think my mum went shopping yesterday, we should be stocked up." I have the console ready and head downstairs to collect the snacks. I'm back in a few minutes.

Horror floods my face when I see Milly's hologram hovering over my bed. She's behind Jackson and I'm sure he hasn't seen her yet. With chips and drinks in my hands, I give them to Jackson as I wave my free hand around behind him trying to make her get back in The Pack. *How the hell did this happen?*

"Thanks. Doritos, yum, haven't had these for a while."

"Yeah, they're a favourite of mine. So, what are we playing?" I ask trying not to sound nervous, because I'm freaking out right now. Milly indicates with her finger that I come closer to her. "Wait," I say under my breath.

"What?"

"Nothing, I'm trying to find a game. Duty Calls, do you know that one?"

"Mate, anything will do, I only play when I'm at friends'

places." He turns to see what I'm doing as I have moved closer to Milly. She's gone instantly and I breathe a sigh of relief. "Oh, found it," I say pulling it out of the bag I had in my hand. "Ok, let's play."

I take my place next to Jackson and start the game while explaining the rules. My breathing is back to normal now Milly's hologram is back in The Pack, but how the hell did it get out?" This is something else I will ask at the next meeting of the alliance.

We're still playing when Trudi messages me to tell me she's out the front. "Trudi is here, be back in a minute." Jackson nods as he grabs another handful of corn chips, the second packet I had opened.

Trudi walks in behind me saying hello to Jackson, "I smell corn chips. Any left?" Jackson hands her the packet that looks empty. "Gee, thanks," she says as she tips the last corn chip and crumbs into her mouth.

"Your fault for being late." Jackson laughs.

"Well some of us have chores to do." She sits on the end of my bed, "So, what are we playing?"

"Here, take my control, you two play for a bit. I have something I need to sort out."

Trudi takes it from me, "Everything ok?"

"Ah, yeah 'course. Just sorting something out for Mum. Won't take long." Thankfully she doesn't keep at me and I sit at the head of my bed texting Sally about Milly's hologram. She answers me quickly telling me not to worry.

Your sister is messing with your head.

She's playing around trying to see how aware you are.

What? I text back, Why?

I don't know for sure, but this happens

when magic is exchanged or inherited.

She wants to know that you don't forget

about The Pack.

Why the hell would I do that? And why did

she do it when there was someone else in
my room?
This time Sally doesn't reply right away.
Oh, you didn't tell me that. Call me, we
can't discuss this via text.
Not right now my friends are here. I'll
call you later.
OK.

I put my phone face down on my bed and go back to chatting with my friends. Whatever Milly is playing at will have to wait until I'm on my own.

TWENTY-ONE

Buster and Community Service

We're walking along our local shopping strip, I'm with Jackson and Trudi when I see him. It's another stinking hot day and we're heading to the movies to sit in air conditioning for a few hours. "Look who's over there." I point over to where Buster is picking up rubbish and placing it in a bag. "He's doing his community service."

Both Jackson and Trudi look across the road. Jackson whistles and Buster looks up at us. His finger is instantly in the air, then he keeps picking up rubbish.

"Leave him alone boys, he's paying for what he did."

"Yeah and so am I. My chin is still sore. I'd like to give him a sucker punch too," Jackson says rubbing his chin. "Hey Buster, working suits you."

"Jackson, stop. We don't need more trouble." Trudi places her hand on his arm.

"Trudi is right, come on let's get out of this heat, the movie will start soon."

Three hours later, we walk out into the late afternoon heat.

Sweat begins forming on my top lip within seconds, the sun is relentless.

"I enjoyed that movie, what did you two think?"

Jackson just shrugs but I say, "A bit predictable, but ok I guess. Of course he was getting the girl in the end."

"Edward, that's why they're called rom-coms, they all have a happy ending."

"Well, I'm choosing the next movie. Come on, I'm dying of heat, let's head home."

We walk towards the park chatting about the next movie choice. Even though this is the long way home, the shade from the trees means it is cooler walking this way.

We're at the section where our group usually meets when Jackson whispers, "Look who's headed our way." Buster, Nate and Artie are walking towards us.

I put both my palms up saying, "Guys, we don't want any trouble. Buster you're in enough shit already."

"Tell your friend to keep his mouth shut then," growls Buster pointing towards Jackson.

"What did I do?" I can see Jackson thinking then he says, "Oh, that comment about you working? That upset you. Buster, I was paying you a compliment. You should feel good that you're helping the community."

By the time Jackson finishes speaking, Buster is standing his ground flanked by Nate and Artie. "Your mouth is too big and gets you in trouble. Apologise and we'll walk away."

"For what? Giving you a compliment." Both Trudi and I grab Jackson by the shoulder trying to stop him but he shrugs us off and throws punches towards Buster with force, anger blaring all over his face. None of them land, luckily for us.

"You weak piece of shit, who taught you to fight?" Buster is laughing and I have grabbed Jackson and pulled him back towards us. "If I wasn't already in trouble doing this community crap, you wouldn't be standing. Come on boys, I've had enough of looking at these idiots, let's go."

I breathe out as I watch the three of them saunter off laughing. "Jackson, are you mad? We're meant to deal with bullies using our brains, not our fists."

Trudi pipes up, "That was reckless, Jackson. It was luck that saved you today, if he wasn't in trouble you'd be in hospital right now with more injuries."

"Ok, ok. I guess I shouldn't have provoked him. I'll see you two soon, I'm going through the short cut back to my place."

We watch as Jackson heads into the bushes where a track has been trampled by everyone who uses this short cut.

I see Buster doing his community service a few times and keep my distance, the last thing I want is to receive one of his punches. One day as I'm riding my bike to buy milk, I see him standing over two boys half his age. The idiot is doing this with shoppers and workers all around him. Does he really want more trouble? As much as I dislike the guy, I am going to help him this time. From behind a tree, I walk towards him as Milly.

"Give me your money, now," he yells at the two younger boys. I can see the fear in their faces as I creep up behind Buster. I nip at his ankle. His scream is ear piercing, did I bite rather than nip? I scamper back to the tree and transform.

"Hey, Buster, you ok?" I'm riding my bike towards him.

"Something bit my ankle, hurts like hell."

I look towards the two boys placing my finger on my lips indicating they remain quiet. "You two go now, I'll look after Buster." Without thinking twice the two boys run off towards the shopping centre.

"I didn't see it but I bet it was that mangy cat."

"Buster, you're delusional, there are no cats around here. Let me have a look at your ankle," I say bending down. "Oh, it doesn't look that bad, you'll be fine."

"Fuck off, Eddie. I can look after myself." He walks off

shoving his finger in the air, his favourite way of saying goodbye.

Back on my bike, I have the milk in a bag hanging off the handlebars and ride home. Buster can't seem to help himself, he's already in trouble but is still bullying kids. When will he learn?

Placing my bike in the garage, I walk in and hand mum the milk. "What took you so long? I was worried."

"Had to save Buster's arse again, that kid is reckless. If he's not careful he'll be in jail before he finishes school."

"What happened this time? Are you hurt?"

"No, Mum, I'm fine. He was bullying two young boys for their money in front of witnesses. See what I mean about being reckless?"

"Hmm, still you shouldn't put yourself in harm's way. I know what he did to Jackson, even though he told me it was an accident. I don't want that happening to you."

I'm surprised she knows. "How did you find out about Jackson being hit?"

"Sweetheart, the gossip network is alive and well. Now take care and stay away from trouble. Thanks for buying the milk." She places it in the fridge as I head upstairs to my room. I know about the gossip network of local mums, they have eyes everywhere. I had better be careful where and how I transform from now on.

TWENTY-TWO

The Next A-Alliance Meeting

I walk into the derelict house to be greeted by Sally. "You didn't call me back. I called you twice, why didn't you answer?"

"Hi Sally, nice to see you again too."

"Oh for goodness…Hello," huffs Sally. "This is serious, the holograms are not meant to be seen by non-magicals."

I pick up a glass and fill it with the cold water in the jug sitting on the bench. "I gathered that trom what you said about not texting, but I haven't been alone long enough to speak to you. Besides, Jackson didn't see Milly, she disappeared as soon as he turned around." I head out towards the others in the backyard. I gasp as I can't believe what I'm seeing. Out in the meadow are more animals. This time I do a double take as two unicorns prance around.

"Yes, they're real in the magic realm."

I ignore Sally and look on at the other animals – as well as the ones I saw last time, there are alpacas, llamas, sheep and animals I don't recognise.

Sally happily points them out, "These are magical creatures too. This little white one that looks like a goat, it's a faun. They help travellers who may be lost in magical forests. The ones over there…" I look towards a group of griffins, these I've seen before in books. "They're griffins and they guard our treasures." She continues pointing out the other mythical animals as we walk toward her parents and say hello. Ester is with them.

"Well, hello again Edward. You have us a little worried about Milly's hologram appearing with a non-magical around."

"I was surprised too, Ester. What can I do about it?"

"We're going to discuss this tonight. Although, I don't think your sister is behind this, she was always diligent and followed our rules. This has happened before but not for many years. Come on, it's time I convene this meeting."

After making ourselves comfortable, I half-listen as Ester goes through the same housekeeping stuff she went through at the last meeting. I stare out to the meadow and see other fascinating creatures. Why are they here and what's their purpose? I know Sally told me what some of them do, but I'm interested in knowing more.

I'm jutted out of my thoughts when Ester calls me to the front.

"You've all met Edward by now, he has a perplexing problem with a hologram of his sister appearing with a non-magical in the room." There are gasps and whispers as Ester asks me to explain exactly what happened, which I do.

Sally's father stands up, "This is dangerous and it hasn't happened since my great-great uncle Charlie let that goblin into his Pack. And we all know what happened then." Again more whispers float around until he puts up his hand to silence everyone. "Our magic was outed and it took us a long time to stop non-magicals from thinking they could perform magic. And worse, the non-magicals were against us, wanted us to denounce our magic saying it was evil."

Ester continues, "Yes that cheeky goblin caused us major problems. We need to find out if he has found his way into Edward's Pack."

Everyone begins talking at once – "It has to be him." "How do we find out?" "That cheeky goblin was a menace."

"Ok, ok. Calm down, let's look at this logically. The goblin was banished by all our top wizards, so he may not be the culprit. All of you are tasked with researching our archives to find any information about him and contact me immediately. We need to get to the bottom of this before another disaster happens."

Ester ushers me back to my chair telling me to wait until she has any information for me. "Try not to worry and maybe don't bring non-magicals too close to your Pack until we know what is going on." I simply nod and sit back down next to Sally and her parents.

For the next two weeks I don't have anyone over, I'm too paranoid they'll see the hologram. When I do see my friends, I'm either out with them or at their homes. Today I'm at Trudi's house in her lounge room, the coolest room. "You seem distracted, are you ok?"

"What? No, I'm fine. Can we concentrate on the movie." We had streamed an old movie, 'Hocus Pocus', which was Trudi's pick. She seems to always pick what we watch.

"Geez, don't bite my head off. I'm not really interested in it, I really asked you over to talk to you about something...umm, but now I don't know if I want to tell you."

I pause the movie and turn towards her. "Trudi, we're friends, you can tell me anything. What's going on with you?"

Her face turns beetroot. "Well, I'm… oh, maybe I'm being silly."

"Will you spit it out."

"I like Jackson. There I said it."

For a moment I'm stunned, then I smile. "Good for you, I think that's wonderful. Two of my good friends making out."

"It's not like that. He has no idea."

"Oh, you haven't told him."

"With his looks, why would he want me? I told you, this is stupid. I have no hope of landing someone like him."

It's true Jackson is good looking, and Trudi is…well she's more on the plain side, but why not? "You haven't even talked to him, how do you know what he thinks of you?"

She looks at me with misty eyes, "How do I tell him? What if he laughs at me?"

I place my arm around her shoulder, "Oh Trudi, you'll never know unless you try. I think he may be flattered. We both know Jackson well, and I don't think he's the type who will laugh at you."

She snuffles and wipes her nose with the back of her hand, "Maybe he won't but maybe he will. Forget I said anything."

"Suit yourself," I shrug. I'm not good at relationship stuff never having been in one, so I decide to end the conversation and put the movie back on. Trudi goes to the kitchen and comes back with cold drinks for both of us. She sits down next to me and we remain silent until the movie ends.

I stand up saying, "Well, I'm off. Catch up tomorrow?"

"Yeah, if I feel like it."

"Trudi don't not come just because Jackson will be there with us, the forecast is for another hot day. Come on, we're all friends."

She doesn't talk until we're at her front door, a whoosh of hot air entering the house. "Ok, I'll come tomorrow, but if you mention one word about…"

I put my hands in the air, "I've forgotten the whole conversation," I say as I head home.

While I'm walking my phone pings. It's a text from Ester, they have worked out why the hologram came out when it shouldn't have. She wants to see me tomorrow. So much for going to the beach.

TWENTY-THREE

Trudi's Surprise

I step off the bus and brave the heat and wind, holding onto my straw hat. The beach is already packed with beachgoers even though it's only ten. I head to the boardwalk and can see Athena and the boys, Athena is waving at me.

When I arrive I ask, "Where's Edward?"

"Had something to do for his mum, he's not coming." Jackson looks up at her squinting, his body sleek with sweat. Trudi's knees go weak as she turns away and places her things near Athena.

Nigel pipes up, "He said he may come later."

"Right, ok. Wonder why he didn't let me know?"

"Probably because he knew I'd tell you. I'm heading in, anyone joining me." Jackson stands up and again Trudi tries not to stare.

"Yep, I'm coming, it's bloody hot." I watch as Nigel and Jackson run towards the shore. Although Nigel is shorter than Jackson, he is as fit and ripped as Jackson is.

"Nice view," laughs Athena. "We're lucky to have nice looking friends."

I smile and only nod, too frightened to say anything, I don't want anyone other than Edward to know how I feel. I first noticed Jackson during the early days of high school, his long legs and taut body catching my eye instantly. At that time I knew I had no hope of being with him, but since then I have looked forward to seeing him every school day and can't believe he is now part to our group.

There have been a few times he has caught me looking at him and he has politely smiled back. I have flushed red each time and turned away from him. As I'm thinking this, he and Nigel come back out of the water. Jackson's muscles glisten in the sun. I turn and fish out my phone and self-consciously start scrolling through the socials.

"You two should go in, the water is clear as. No seaweed or blue bottles today."

"I'm hot now, come on Trudi, let's go in." I put my phone back in my bag and follow Athena, I need cooling down now.

We're in the water only a few minutes when the boys come back in. "Hey, Athena, want to get on my shoulders?"

"Yeah, great. Come on Trudi, you get on Jackson's shoulders."

Before I can answer, Jackson is next to me and ducks under the water. I have no choice but to sit on his shoulders. My measured heartbeat is suddenly escalated to frenetic as I feel his hands on my shins. I am conscious of his shoulders under me feeling the warmth of him, his shoulders burned on top of his existing tan.

"Are you scared, Trudi. The look on your face is priceless."

"Nah, I'm fine. Just finding my balance." I hope I sound calmer than I feel.

Athena laughs, "Right then, come closer, let's have a water fight." Nigel and she move closer and Athena begins to splash water over me while laughing. I fall off into the surf, not because Athena was splashing me, but because I wanted to get off Jackson's shoulders.

"Wow, that was easy. Jump on again, see if you can do the same."

I'm treading water and ducking under the waves. When I come up I say, "I've had enough, going back now. It was fun." I swim back to the shore leaving Anthea still on Nigel's shoulders as she laughs at something Jackson has said.

When I'm back on my towel I watch my friends' body surf and laugh with each other. I wish Edward was here because I am more comfortable being around Jackson with Edward as a buffer. I am thinking about leaving when I hear Buster's booming voice.

"Well, if it isn't Eddie's girlfriend." I turn to see him with Artie and Nate. I turn away without responding, he continues, "What's with you, you snob. Can't even say hello." Before I can respond, Jackson is back and picks up his towel.

"Piss off, Buster."

"What? Jus' saying hello and she's being rude."

"Go and find a spot without causing trouble will ya. We're here to enjoy ourselves," says Nigel as he walks up behind Jackson.

"Oh, lookey here, he has back up. Where's Eddie? We can make this even."

"We're not making anything," says Nigel, "go and do what Jackson told you to do."

"Who made him my boss?" asks Buster making a move to come closer.

"Buster stop, you're still doing community service, do you really want to get into trouble again?" Jackson stands his ground and I can see he's ready for a fight.

"Stop, all of you," I say, "Hello, Buster. Are you happy now."

"Too late now bitch."

Jackson moves forward slapping a huge punch onto Buster's jaw. "I said go and find a spot, leave us alone. Want me to call the lifeguards so you can get into more trouble?"

Nate and Alfie try to help Buster up but he shrugs them off. "I can get up by meself," he blurts out with a trickle of blood going down his chin. "You wait until I've finished community service, Jack. Let's go boys." He waves his arm and he and his two friends walk away, Buster holding his towel up to his chin.

Athena goes up to Jackson, "Well done for protecting Trudi."

"Yeah, well he was the one being rude. You ok, Trudi?"

I look up at him with a weak smile, "I'm fine, you didn't have to punch him, he would have walked away when you mentioned the lifeguards."

"Maybe, but it felt good punching him again." Jackson beams a huge smile at me and my heart skips a beat. My feelings for him are too much now, I'm going to tell him how I feel the next time we're alone. Being on his broad shoulders in the water confirmed I need to know if he feels the same way.

An hour later, the midday sun is too hot to handle so we decide to head for the kiosk and buy food. There is shade around where we can sit out of the sun. The boys buy burgers and chips, Athena a salad and I decide on grilled fish and salad. If I'm going to impress Jackson I'm going to have to look my best. From now on only healthy food and maybe an exercise routine. I will also ask my mother to help me with looking after my skin, this acne has to go.

I'm sitting on the grass when Jackson sits next to me. I feel the heat coming off his body and try not to blush. "Umm, thanks for sticking up for me."

"Sure, always. That Buster needs to be put in his place." Again that beaming smile, this time all for me.

I look around wondering where Athena and Nigel are.

"They've gone back to where our towels are, Athena was worried someone might steal something."

"Ah, ok. Maybe we should go back too?" I look right into his eyes, then turn quickly away. We haven't been on our own this long before. I am giddy, nervous and happy all at the same time.

"Nah, I don't want to eat in the sun. Besides, isn't this nice, just the two of us?"

"Erm, I guess so." I simply eat my food and say nothing else, bathing in the moment of Jackson saying, 'the two of us'.

He is quiet as he eats as well. When he has finished, he puts out his hand for me to give him my rubbish, "You finished?" I hand him my half-eaten fish, I was too excited to finish it.

"You eat like a bird," Jackson laughs as he stands up. With the rubbish in the bin, I watch as he walks back towards me. My eyes take in his physique and I don't realise I am staring until he says, "I do work out, this doesn't come easily."

"I'm sorry…I didn't realise…"

He keeps laughing, "Trudi, I've noticed you staring before, it's ok." He puts out his hand to help her up and I take it without hesitating. Jackson gives me a peck on the cheek, "I'm flattered." I do everything in my power not to kiss him back. "I'm ready for another swim, are you?" He starts running back to our spot leaving me to watch him wondering what the hell just happened… and feeling wonderfully giddy.

TWENTY-FOUR

The Goblin and The Pack

There is only Ester and I at the A-Alliance house. It is eerily quiet and I notice there are no animals out in the meadow. "Where are the animals?"

"Oh, they only come to the meadow when we are around. Some of them are orphans of people who have passed, they are waiting for a new magical to pick them as their animal. This house remains derelict and empty when we're not here."

I'm confused. "But we're here now?"

"Sorry, I mean when most of us are here. They won't bother coming just to be with two of us. Now, we have no more time to waste, did you bring your Pack?"

I wanted to ask where the animals go if they're not in the meadow? But I sensed that Ester wanted to get on with what was in my Pack that shouldn't be there. I hand it to her and she begins mumbling as soon as she has it in her hands. I try to make out what she is saying but she is speaking in another language, not one I've heard before. After five minutes she returns The Pack to me.

"There you go, you shouldn't have any more problems with that little rascal."

"Umm, thanks. That's it, are you sure he's gone?"

"We did a lot of research and found the incantation that rids The Pack of unwanted nasties. Luckily, you had a somewhat nuisance goblin who was having a laugh, he won't trouble you further."

"Ok, thanks Ester, this was easier than I thought. You were all so worried."

"We were, but as it turns out, this goblin is a descendent of the original rascal, he's a nephew and quite harmless. Now, shall we go, you can still make it to the beach if you like."

I follow her as she steps out the front door and locks it behind her. As nobody other than us magicals come here, I'm not sure why it needs to be locked. I don't bother asking though, Ester seems on a mission to get out of here.

An hour later I'm in my room, I wasn't in the mood to go to the beach. With the fan in the corner, my room is cool and I'm happy to chill out on my own. My eyes are heavy, I'm about to dose off when my phone pings. It's Trudi.

Coming over, have something wonderful to tell you.

Great, I wanted to be on my own and I'm about to text her back but decide against it because I'm curious now. It will take her thirty minutes to get here, so I doze until I hear the doorbell.

"Hi, wait till you hear what happened at the beach." She starts talking as soon as she's in the door and doesn't stop, her excitement blurts out with her words, "Jackson, I think he likes me. We spent a few minutes alone together and he said he's seen me staring at him and he doesn't mind that I do."

"And from those few minutes you know this how?"

Trudi gives me a perplexed look, "Because he was sweet and I sensed it, he didn't have to say anything more."

I sigh and think before I speak not wanting to upset her. "I'm happy for you… and him. But I wouldn't get my hopes up until he actually does something. You two haven't even kissed."

"I rushed over here to tell you and now you doubt me? Thanks for your vote of confidence. And he gave me a kiss on the cheek."

"On the cheek doesn't count. Boys can be sweet to their friends, that doesn't mean they want something more. You liking him is making you *hope* he likes you." I watch as she sits gingerly on my bed, guiding herself with her hand. She is visibly upset.

"I suppose you're right. He's always been sweet to me… to all of us."

"Your sixth sense may be right…" I stop talking when Milly's hologram appears behind Trudi.

"Edward, are you ok? You look like you've seen a ghost."

I whisper to the hologram to get back in the Pack.

Trudi turns, "Who are you talking to? Oh my… Milly!"

I look at Trudi and talk fast, "It's not her, just a hologram. You're not supposed to be seeing this."

"Yes she is." It's the hologram talking but in a shrill high-pitched voice, almost childlike. "I'm here to help you beat those bullies."

Trudi and I look at each other with wide-eyed fascination. "Who are you?"

"My name is Leafia, I'm Milly's friend and she told me she wants me to help you in your quest."

"Are you the nephew of…"

"Niece, actually. Ester and her crew got that part wrong. That's why the incantation she used didn't work on me, it's for male goblins. Now, I know you told Trudi about your magic, Edward, so I'm not going to cause problems because she can see me. No other non-magical will see me."

Ok, that's fine, but why did you appear while Jackson was here?"

"My mistake, sorry. I'm new at this and didn't realise it

was him until he turned around. Now, I have some ideas on how I can help you with Buster."

The hologram changes to Leafia's image, she is a tiny elf-like being with pointy ears wearing a red dress and red spangly shoes. We watch on and listen. After speaking to us for ten minutes, Leafia returns to The Pack leaving Trudi and I amazed at her suggestions.

"Woah, what just happened?"

"Trudi, you're not to tell anyone about this. So many magical rules have been broken this afternoon." Before she can answer, we hear Mum calling. "Up here Mum, Trudi is here too." Within minutes she is at my door.

"Hello, you two. Had a good day? Dinner will be ready in an hour, Edward," says Vanessa looking directly at Trudi. "Are you staying Trudi?"

"Ah, no thanks Mrs Shipley, I was just about to head home." Trudi begins to move towards the door and Mum let's her pass.

"See you tomorrow Trudi, we'll talk more then." She doesn't acknowledge me and I hope like all hell she keeps quiet.

TWENTY-FIVE

The Extraordinary Meeting

I organised a meeting at the park with everyone from the gang attending, except two who were away on holiday. "Thanks for coming and taking time out of your break, we wanted to let you know this information before we go back to school, it's going to help all of us." I'm nervous, my hands clammy with sweat. I look towards Trudi who indicates I keep going. "We've been given some extra ideas on dealing with Buster and any other bullies we encounter. One of these ideas is out there, maybe even a bit harsh on our part, so we'll keep this one for extreme occasions."

I'm about to keep talking when Jackson arrives and stands next to us. "Sorry I'm late. Keep going."

"Yeah, get on with it, Edward, we want to know what you're blabbering about." Nigel turns around with his arms out including everyone in his gesture. A few nod their heads looking towards me.

"Ok, Okay! The two ideas we can use without causing too much commotion is – one, stay calm and ask the bully how would they feel if the situation was reversed? A bit of reverse psychology. When the bully is thinking about this bit of wisdom, run. Fast. There will be someone dealing with the bully." What I'm not saying is that Leafia will be wisping around invisibly, shouting "bullying makes you look small".

"Oh sure, like Buster is going to stop pounding me long enough for me to say that." Nigel smirks.

Trudi looks towards him, "We're not saying it will always work. Keep listening and wait until Edward finishes before commenting."

I continue, "Thanks Trudi. The second idea is – cover your face and conjure happy thoughts. Let the bully rant then step back if you can. You'll find the bully won't be able to touch you."

"Oh please," Nigel scoffs, "Where did this *foolproof* idea come from? Edward, stop wasting our time." There are murmurs and more comments from the others in the gang.

"Trust me, there will be a force between you and the bully, let's just say it's magic." And it will, Leafia, invisible again, will be there dealing with the bully.

This time it's Athena who speaks in mocking tones, "What the hell are you on? This is crazy talk."

I'm beginning to become frustrated with the interruptions and it shows in my voice, "For fuck's sake, will you just listen and trust that it will work. Haven't things worked up till now?" There are more murmurs and a few nods as I keep going, "I won't take up too much more of your time, but please stop interrupting so we can all go home." This time the anger in my voice keeps everyone quiet.

"There is one final idea and it involves self-defence lessons. I'm organising lessons with the local gym for any of you who are up for learning how to protect yourself. If you feel that you are in danger, and once you are proficient enough, you can use the methods learned to disable the bully. Think kicking in places that really hurt." Again, Leafia will be in the background if needed to tell the bully not to retaliate. If they do, there will be consequences.

"This is more practical, I'm up for those," says Nigel, "but what happens next time? Bullies have long memories, I don't think this will scare them for long."

"Trust me, that's all I'm going to say about your doubts. You're free to go everyone, send me a message if you'd like to join the self-defence class."

It's not long before only the five of us are left in the park. Jackson is the first to speak, "Ok, what's going on, where did these far-fetched ideas come from? Magic, are you kidding me?"

He, Nigel and Athena are staring at me waiting for an answer. How do I explain Leafia's magic without sounding like a nutjob? I try my best. "We have to think differently, take on the bullying from different angles. Ok, maybe magic was not the right word."

"You're damned right it's not. Honestly, I think you've lost it, Edward."

"Easy Nigel," says Trudi, "you've been negative this whole time. Haven't we made progress with the bullies and we have a teacher on our side too."

"Suppose so," whispers Nigel.

"Yeah, give Edward a break. Without him all of you would have no hope against the bullies." I smile at Jackson thankful he is on my side too. My phone begins pinging with members of the gang interested in joining in the self-defence lessons.

The self-defence classes start a week after the meeting. Because the whole gang decided to join, the gym gave us a discount on the fees. I know this is going to be money well spent.

For the next four weeks we will spend two nights a week doing basic training, enough to keep us out of trouble. By the time school starts in February, we will have finished the course.

After the first lesson, Trudi comments as we're walking out of the gym. "I'm so unfit but I know these skills I'm learning will be worth it."

Jackson nods, "We're all going to benefit."

As long as the bullies don't retaliate." This is negative Nigel again. I gave him that nickname.

"Ladies and gentlemen, Negative Nigel is at it again."

"Shut it, Edward." The five of us laugh with Athena slapping Nigel on the back.

"You like to give shit but can't take it, Nigel. Man up, will you."

We're all still laughing as we head towards the waiting cars ready to take us home. Mum asks what's so funny. "Oh, just Nigel again, we call him Negative Nigel now."

Mum laughs and proceeds to tell me a story of how negative my Dad was when they first met. Apparently he was a geek at school and would be very proud of what I have achieved. "Keep going, Edward, you're doing a good thing. Hungry?"

"Starving, I could murder a burger right now."

"Hmm, adrenaline has kicked in I see, maybe murder is a bit strong a word?" I smile at her as she heads towards our favourite burger joint.

TWENTY-SIX

The New School Year

The day before school starts, I'm at a special A-Alliance meeting with Ester, Sally and her parents, as well as Leafia. We're sitting in the kitchen discussing how much Leafia is actually allowed to do. "Thanks for allowing this, Ester, I know allowing Leafia into the non-magical world is unusual, but I promise we will be careful."

"You must be careful, Edward. Leafia cannot stay invisible for long. This is a skill she has only just learned."

I'm surprised to hear this. "You didn't mention this, Leafia?"

"Stop worrying, I know what I'm doing. I've used my invisibility more than you know, Ester. The non-magical world is familiar to me. Remember that I'm the one who taught Milly how to transform into a cat."

"We know you taught Milly as well as protected her, Leafia, but you still must be careful." This time it's Sally's father who is warning us.

I listen as Ester continues explaining the rules to keep our magic safe from being discovered. Having learned so much since becoming a part of this secret society, I will do everything in my power to keep things secret.

The first school week passes without incident and I'm hoping Buster and the rest of his crew has learned a lesson. I walk into the science lab and see Mr Ferris, greeting him. He acknowledges me but doesn't speak until everyone is settled.

"Welcome back all of you, I trust you had a good break and are ready for Year 8." Ignoring the few mutters of discontent amongst his students, he starts the lesson.

When the double lesson is finished, I run into Jackson, who, along with Buster, is now in Year 11 at the lockers. "Hey, things have been quiet?"

"Hey, Edward. Yeah, the calm before the storm maybe?"

"Hmm, maybe. Or Buster has grown up."

"Unlikely," laughs Jackson throwing his backpack over his shoulder, "You ready for some chips?" I nod and follow him towards the school gates.

The queue at the fish shop is long as usual, we join the end of it. As Jackson and I chat, we hear the usual brash voice of Buster behind us. "If it isn't my two faves, Jack and Eddie. Look boys, the two love birds are here." He indicates to Nate and Artie who are standing behind him.

I whisper to Jackson to ignore him but know this is not going to end well. Buster has been too quiet.

"Sorry, what was that? What are you whispering to your lover?"

Before I can stop him, Jackson is standing in front of Buster. Jackson is now a good head taller than him and cuts an imposing figure. "Where the hell has this come from? Now we're gay? Buster you're full of shit."

"You're a bit lankier, aren't ya? But ya don't scare me, now back off."

"I will if you stop with the gay slurs. You know we're straight."

Buster stands on his toes, "Do I? You two were chummy during the holidays and have been since Jack here decided to be besties with you, Eddie."

"Give it a break, we're in Year 11 now, when are you going to grow up?" Jackson's anger shows as I place my hand on his shoulder but he shrugs it off.

"I'll grow up when I'm ready and you can't tell me what to do." Buster walks away asking his two mates to follow him, "Let's get some chips, I'm starving."

Jackson and I watch on as the three of them push into the front of the line. "He hasn't learned anything."

"No, but leave it, Jackson. He was just stirring you up waiting for you to take the bait."

"I know," he says as we move up the line.

The next day I'm at my locker when I see Buster is with a Year 7 boy holding up his backpack as the young boy fills it with the snacks his parents have given him. "There's a good kid," says Buster patting his head. "Keep bringing these for me and you'll be safe, I'll make sure of it."

His empty promises anger me. This poor kid just needs to forget his snacks for one day and he'll pay for it. I remember when this happened to me during my first few weeks in Year 7, forgetting to bring chips for Buster cost me that day. I went home with sore ribs after he showed me how not to forget again. I wait until Buster walks away before making sure the boy is ok and let him know to come to me if he ever needs help. He gives me a wane smile, his fear is obvious.

Lunchtime is the next time I see Buster bothering the same boy. My anger wells up, isn't it enough the boy is giving up his snacks. I'm in the canteen line with Jackson and Trudi. "Not again," I say out loud.

"What?" asks Trudi.

"Buster, he was bothering that kid this morning. Took his snacks, now he wants more from him."

"That's not fair," says Jackson who storms towards Buster placing his hand on his shoulder pushing him around.

"What the...? oh it's you. Mind your own business." Buster turns back to the boy.

"Leave him alone, wasn't this morning enough?"

"What's it to you? I'm a growing boy who needs food."

Jackson is about to throw a punch when Mr Ferris stops him. "Enough, Jackson. Buster come with me." We watch on wondering what our teacher has in store for him.

We soon find out. With our lunches in our hands, we walk out of the canteen to see Buster picking up rubbish. He scowls at us as we laugh. He deserves everything he gets. Not that I think this will stop him from bullying.

And it doesn't. At the end of the next school day, Buster is standing over one of our gang members, screaming at the top of his lungs. The next thing that happens is the best thing I've seen happen to Buster. Our friend raises his knee and Buster collapses in front of him grasping at his groin.

I feel Leafia whooshing past me. "And that's one. Self-defence 101 is working already."

Over the next few months, Leafia helps out with great success. The bullies have no idea what is going on and we geeks are enjoying the days without bullying.

TWENTY-SEVEN

Leafia Shows the Bullies

Every time Leafia helps out a kid being bullied, Buster is weakened, as is his crew. They need time to regroup as they try to work out this thing that seems to come between them and their victim.

We geeks bask in the glow of the reduced bullying. Nigel even apologies to me for not believing that the *magic* would work. "Mate, I was negative, you were right. Seeing these bullies squirm is priceless."

"Thanks, but this may make them want revenge, we need to be careful we're not pushing too hard."

"They're the ones pushing too hard, Edward," says Trudi after taking a bite of her sandwich, her words muffled by her chewing. "Shit, sorry, I should have waited until I swallowed. But you know what I mean, Buster never seems to want to give up."

I smile at her, "I know, but can you imagine how bad things will be if we infuriate him to the point of no return? He could easily hurt someone again. Remember the kid with the broken nose?"

My friends all nod. "Well, so far we're doing ok," says Jackson, "but you're right Edward, we should be careful. I've seen how stupidly angry Buster can become, he's not reasonable when he's in that mood." The bell chimes signalling the end of lunchtime, "See you all later and we can breathe a little more because Buster seems to be laying low right now." The others acknowledge Jackson and head to their respective classrooms.

Everyone is waiting for me at the school gate. "Sorry guys, I was talking to Mr Ferris about my science assignment."

"No problem, we were discussing what we talked about at lunchtime," says Jackson. Before anyone else can answer an almighty scream is heard. "What the hell? That sounded like it was coming from the toilet block." The five of us head in that direction.

"I'm not bullshitting, I saw this thing, looked like a goblin with a red dress and spangly shoes. She was telling me not to retaliate after this kid kicked me in the shin and then ran off. At first it was just a voice, but then she appeared right before my eyes." Buster is bewildered and still yelling. Nate and Artie are watching on along with Stella and Beth.

"A goblin? Are you delusional, Buster?" says Stella.

"You don't believe me either? I swear I saw her and then when I screamed she disappeared in a puff."

I'm hearing all this and panic begins attacking my body, I try to control my breathing. Leafia assured me she would stay invisible, what the hell went wrong this time? I think quickly trying to explain the situation in logical terms, "Buster, are you sure it wasn't the kid's little sister? She was probably trying to help out her brother."

"You too, Edward? I know what I saw, it wasn't a normal human. Her ears were pointy, her nose was squashed into her face, all I could see was nostril. And, she had one green eye and one blue. Explain that?"

His crew murmur and move closer to Buster, Nate placing his hand on this shoulder. "Come on mate, let's get you home."

"No, I want to know what the hell happened, you geeks know something about this, don't ya? What are you playing at?"

I speak before anyone because I need to control this situation, "Buster, what makes you think we're behind this? I don't even know what a goblin looks like."

"Well I do now. And if I see her again I'll have my phone ready to take a photo. Then everyone will believe me."

That's the last thing we need, a photo of Leafia will confirm the existence of magic in our community. Rumours have been rife on and off for years with some people saying they saw magical creatures, just as Buster has now. "Look, none of us can explain what happened here, it's best we go home, we all have assignments to finish." Buster starts walking towards the gates mumbling under his breath with his crew following. I start heading in the same direction when Trudi stops me.

"Edward wait a minute." I stop while the others keep walking. "What are we going to do about this?"

"We? You can't do anything, I'll have to talk to the other magicals to sort this out. You're not even supposed to know about Leafia."

"Well I do and I want to help."

"Thanks, I appreciate that. Let me see once I've spoken to the others, if we need your help I'll let you know."

That evening I'm on a video chat with Sally and Ester. I called Sally first but she said we needed to include Ester as this was a serious breach of the magical rules. "I feel awful, this would not have happened if I hadn't involved Leafia."

"From what you've told us it seems Leafia does as she

pleases, besides she assured all of us she would not materialise in front of non-magicals."

"I know, Ester, but you were worried as she is still learning about being invisible."

"I was and as it turns out I was right to be. We have to stop Leafia being involved with your quest to fight the bullies. Are you sure this Buster you speak of is the only person who saw her?"

"I think so, the kid he was bullying ran off after kicking him in the shin. Leafia appeared after the kid was gone."

"Ok, then this is good. It seems to me that no one believed Buster, right?"

"Yes and as I explained, I tried to use logic and say it was the kid's sister."

"Good, very good. So, we need to minimise the damage by firstly banishing Leafia from the non-magical world and secondly assure Buster he didn't see anything."

Sally speaks, "Banishing Leafia is the easy part, but convincing Buster is harder."

"Let me have a think about it, I'm sure I can find a spell that will help him forget. I'll need to make sure everyone else who saw is case with this spell, it's going to be a lot of work. But that is mine and Leafia's problem. Now, it's late and you two should both be in bed. Good evening and leave all this to me."

Sally stays on the chat with me for a few more minutes reassuring me that Ester will find a solution, spells to make people forget are plentiful.

"I'm glad to hear that, thanks Sally. Enjoy the rest of your night." She clicks off the chat and I place my laptop on top of my bookshelf next to my bed. The exhaustion hits me the minute I put my head on my pillow, what a day!

TWENTY-EIGHT

Buster Forgets

I am still ranting about what I saw. "She was there, right in front of me, standing in her red shoes, her feet together." I keep going on and on as Nate says goodbye when he reaches his house.

"See you on Monday, Buster and make sure you get some rest."

The other gang members are already at their homes, my place is the furthest from school. I push the rickety gate open careful not to get a splinter. My mum's house is falling apart even though my stepdad tries to fix things. He's useless but we don't have the money to get a proper job done.

When I'm inside my mother asks where I've been. "Had to stay back at school. What's for dinner?"

"Meatloaf. Be ready in twenty minutes."

"Again! We've had meatloaf already this week."

"Stop ya whining, when you can pay for the food you can choose what's for dinner."

I walk to my room hating the fact we're poor. My real dad

was a gambler and lost most of his pays on the horses. He'd come home drunk and abuse Mum and occasionally he'd turn on me too. I had hated him and my stepdad isn't much better, although he doesn't gamble. This is only because the lazy sod doesn't work, Mum works at a supermarket stacking shelves, this is our only income.

I remember when my dad died Mum told me to keep studying and stay at school because only a decent education will get me out of this poverty cycle. Only two terms left this year and then the following one is my final year. I can't wait to finish school so I can leave this hell hole of a house.

Monday morning arrives and I'm running late for school. There had been no hot water for a shower so I'd gone to Nate's place for a hot shower. This added an extra twenty minutes to my morning routine. My mood is darker than midnight and I am ready for anyone who challenges me today.

Arriving at school, I'm putting things in my locker when Stella says good morning. "How are you this morning?"

"Fine, why?"

"Just askin', being polite."

"Sure, ok." I make a move to go to class but she stops me.

"The kid you bullied on Friday has gone to Mr Ferris."

"Has he now? Well I'm prepared to talk to Mr Ferris, he doesn't scare me."

"I know that Buster, but don't go saying stupid things like seeing goblins."

I look at Stella and laughs, "What the fuck you talkin' about?"

Stella looks surprised. "Oh nothin', forget I said anything. See you at lunchtime."

I head to my classroom wondering what the hell Stella was on about. I decide to forget about her and start to formulate the lie I'm going to tell Mr Ferris. The kid kicked my shin, I didn't hurt the kid at all.

Science class ends with Mr Ferris calling me over, "I've had another complaint about you, you want to tell me what happened last Friday afternoon."

I don't answer until all the students have left the lab. "Oh yeah, who complained?"

"You know who I'm talking about. His father is a doctor and made a complaint to the principal after his son spoke to me. Apparently this is not the first time you've bothered this boy."

"He's lying. I walked into the toilets as he was coming out and without me doing anythin' he kicked me in the shin, look." I show him the bruise.

"Hmm, that's a shiny one but I don't believe you Buster, you didn't do anything to provoke the attack?"

"Sir, you know since I did all that community work I've been good, no more bullying for me." Mr Ferris acknowledges that he hasn't heard of me bullying anyone lately, but I know this is only because no one else has complained. Most of the kids are scared of me and my crew.

Mr Ferris lets out a sigh, "Fine, go home Buster but if I get another complaint you will know about it. Next time I won't be so lenient."

Saturday morning is raining, the sort of soaking rain that makes you want to stay in bed, which is where I am. I'm scrolling through the socials seeing what everyone else is up to. Deciding that nothing special is happening, I throw on a hoodie and head to the kitchen.

"Afternoon sleepyhead."

"Had nothin' to get up for. Besides, it's only eleven." I answer my stepdad with the disdain he deserves. "Where's Mum?"

"She was called in to do extra shifts this weekend." As soon as he says this I remember that she had told me that. This will please my freeloading stepfather because there'll be more money in the bank this week.

I look around the kitchen – dirty dishes in the sink, cereal boxes left open on the old table, my mother's coffee cup still with some left. I know it's up to me to tidy up before Mum arrives home or she'll lose it. My shithead stepdad won't do it.

"Make sure you clean up," says my stepdad.

I begin to rage inside, how dare he tell me what to do. "Who are you to tell me what to do?" I stand tall and face him.

"You will do what you are told, I'm the head of this house when your mother isn't here." Without flinching, my stepdad attacks, a slap crashes across my face catching me off guard.

"What the fuck was that for?"

"You had better shut it before I do worse," says my stepdad walking away holding a steaming cup of coffee.

The rain is relentless all day so I stay home. It was eight o'clock when I remember I hadn't eaten dinner. Walking into the kitchen my stepdad is there again, I had avoided him all day.

"What's for dinner? I'm starved." His words are slurred.

I can smell the booze on his breath, four beer bottles empty on the table. "Get your own."

This was enough to trigger him, my stepdad grabs me by the t-shirt. "Didn't you hear me this morning, I'm the boss and if I say I'm hungry, you prepare. Got it?"

I pull at his hand but he has a firm grip. His left hand comes up and slaps me again. "Answer back again and you'll get more of that."

Suddenly, a ginger cat is clawing at his leg, my stepdad yells in pain. "Who let that in? Where did it come from?" With this he lets go of me and I step back towards the kitchen sink. I fish around for something in the sink. Finding a knife, I point it towards my stepdad.

"Get away from me, you freeloading arsehol'. When Mum

comes home I'm going to tell her you attacked me. You're out of 'ere, I've had enough."

He glares at me, "Put the knife down before someone gets hurt, you idiot. And get this cat out of here." He hobbles to the bathroom to attend to his leg.

I look down at the cat who seems to be grinning. "I suppose I should say thanks. How *did* you get in here?" Opening the front door, which had been locked, I allow the cat to walk out. "Haven't seen you around lately but go home now before I decide to do something you won't be happy about.

TWENTY-NINE

The A-Alliance Mid-Year Meeting

I'm patting a miniature horse that is at the edge of the meadow. "You're a friendly thing, aren't you?" The horse keeps rubbing his nose against my hand as Sally comes up to say hello.

"I see you've met Milly's friend. This is Cinnamon."

"Hi Sally," I say turning towards her. "Oh, this was Milly's horse?"

"Sort of. When Milly was ill, Cinnamon stayed close to her and kept her company. They became friends and Cinnamon was always here when Milly was around."

"Well, let me introduce myself, I'm Edward, Milly's twin." The horse nods his head as if he knows what I'm talking about. Sally notices my confusion.

"He knows who you are. He came up to you, right?" I nod. "Cinnamon wants to be your friend too."

"That's nice, thanks Cinnamon. I'm happy to be your friend." I feel weird telling a horse he's my friend but I have the feeling he and all the animals in the meadow know what we humans are saying.

"We'd better go and sit down, Ester is about to start this mid-year meeting."

We take our seats next to Sally's parents and wait for Ester to begin. Sally had filled me in on what is special about this meeting, one where every magical has to attend. Ester focuses on the good deeds and what has been achieved so far this year.

"Many of you have assisted the non-magicals with their difficulties and I, along with the rest of the committee, thank you. Of particular mention is Edward Shipley." She indicates I come up on the podium. I have no idea why I've been singled out.

"Edward, as Milly the Cat, did a selfless deed only a few nights ago. He helped a bully from being hurt badly by his stepfather, one who has bullied Edward many times,." There is light applause and I feel my face reddening. "When someone is your enemy it takes courage to help them out. Edward, we thank you for being the better person." She indicates I go back to my seat as there is more applause. When the applause has died down, Ester continues, "From what I hear this isn't the first time you've helped out your nemesis. Good work."

Half an hour later after Ester has thanked many others and gone through what needs to be done in the next six months, we all congregate around the massive tables of food. There is twice as much tonight than at other meetings. "There are many more of us to feed," says Sally.

She is right, as I look around I see people in robes, probably wizards, some are in a type of uniform and others are dressed like us. "What's with the uniform?"

"Oh, they're from overseas – New Zealand, America and some from Europe. They are part of a special group of magicals who have descendants going back generations. For instance, Milly was the first in your family to have powers, right?" Again I just nod. "Well, these magicals have family going back to the time of ancient Rome and Greece. They are like royalty."

"Amazing. I hadn't thought about that. How far back does your family go?"

"My parents are the second generation, I'm third. We're not quite in their league yet. Come on, I'll introduce you."

Before I can protest, Sally calls over to a group not far from us. "Let me introduce you to Edward Shipley, he is Milly's twin."

There are five in the group and they all offer their hands for me to shake. One is the oldest and his uniform is adorned with medals, two are middle-aged and the youngest two, a boy and a girl, are only just older than me. "Thank you, it's nice to meet you all too."

"We've been hearing a lot about you, Edward. You are doing good things at your school." This is the older one, who I assume is the grandfather.

"Well, thanks but I'm not doing it all on my own. We formed a group and together we help others being bullied." We continue talking and I find out where they live and all the good deeds they do. They even invite me to visit them one day in America, they live in California. That would be a dream for me, I've never been outside of Australia.

Ester calls us all to listen, "Thank you everyone for attending this mid-year meeting, it's time we all went home and I look forward to seeing the local magicals at the next meeting. For everyone who came from overseas, safe travels and we'll see you next year."

I'm on the bus home and think about what I've learned tonight. First, I made a new friend and it's a horse and secondly, I met an amazing family of magicals. I am in awe at what my life looks like now and it's all thanks to Milly bestowing me her magic. I miss her every day but when I use her magic I feel close to her, my little sister by only five minutes.

No one knows about these meetings or The Pack, not even Trudi. She knows about Leafia but doesn't know where she came from. She did ask but I avoided the question. Now that Leafia is no longer around, Trudi has stopped asking. And my mother, all she knows is that I can transform into Milly the Cat. Will I tell them more as I learn more? This remains to be seen.

THIRTY

Another Year Ends

We're walking out of the school gates heading to another summer holiday break. Next year Jackson is in year 12 and is excited about his future. "I'm looking at universities but I may take a gap year, I haven't decided yet."

"How exciting, university." Trudi turns and is walking backwards as she talks directly to Jackson. "I'm going to university too, to study economics." Trudi is trying to impress Jackson having told me she still likes him although Jackson has never made a move.

"Impressive Trudi, you already know what you want to do. I'm still deciding so it may turn into a gap year. Not sure if I want to do architecture, graphic design or engineering."

"They're all impressive too," I say, "no idea what I want to do, I want to concentrate on these next school years, nothing thrills me yet career wise." I watch on as Trudi flirts with Jackson, it's just the three of us, the others are already home. It's cute what she is doing, talking about the courses he can follow online before he decides. She hasn't a hope in hell with him, especially once he's out of school and meets all the Uni babes.

We arrive at Trudi's house before she realises I'm still with them. "Did you want something, Edward?"

"Nah, just wanted to stretch my legs a little further." This is a lie because I need to speak with Jackson, on his own. "See you around." I keep walking with Jackson towards his house.

I start asking him about Buster, who had been quite ruthless the latter part of this year. Nate and Artie were following his lead too. "What's gotten into him this time?"

"Who knows? Even Mr Ferris' anti-bullying classes don't seem to be working. I'm afraid you all have another year of him and his antics."

Jackson arrives at his house and turns to me, "Why didn't you talk about this in front of Trudi? She might have some ideas too."

"Ah, I know. I… umm, wanted to talk to you about her, you know she likes you right?"

"Yeah, I've noticed. She's a nice girl as a friend and that's all. I don't want anything to complicate my life, I want to concentrate on my future. Although she is looking prettier lately. Is it me or have you noticed too?"

"I don't want her to get her hopes up, so I was just checking. And yes, I have noticed that her skin is clearer and she is fitter, she has told me she is exercising more."

"You keen, Edward?"

"Me? No, she's a good friend, that's all. Same as you. And don't mention I said anything, she'll be pissed because I promised I wouldn't."

"Don't worry, mate, I won't spill. See you around, ok?"

"Sure," I say as I walk back to my place. I feel sorry for Trudi but I knew the answer before I asked Jackson.

The five of us are at the beach on the day after New Year's. Over the Christmas break, Nigel and Athena had hooked-up, which wasn't a surprise, they had been keen on each other for some time. Jackson had decided to take a gap year and travel, leaving Trudi and I with no plans other than to finish school.

"I have plans," says Trudi in a huff, "I'm studying economics at Uni."

"That's right, I forgot. Ok, then I'm the only one without a plan." I laugh as we settle ourselves down on our towels. We had opted for an afternoon swim today as a storm had been predicted in the morning, which never eventuated.

"Hey, did you know there's a concert on the boardwalk at six? Athena and I are hanging around to see what it's like, what about you guys?"

"Sounds good, Nigel," says Jackson as does Trudi.

"Sorry, no can do. My mum needs me to do things with her. Next time." I hate that I lie to my friends when I'm going to see magicals, but I can't tell them the truth. Sally and her parents have invited me to their house for dinner. I'm interested to see what a magical household looks like.

Jackson and Nigel head towards the water, "Come on Edward, the girls aren't warm enough yet, but we're ready for a dip," yells Nigel.

We're only in the water for a few minutes when I come up after ducking under a wave to see Buster near the girls. "Hey guys, there's trouble brewing."

"Not again," says Jackson, "when will he learn." The three of us run towards the girls as we hear Buster laughing.

"Oh look, the three amigos are here to rescue you, how nice."

"What's so funny, Buster?" Jackson is standing over him as Buster takes the smile off his face.

"Nothin'. Just tellin' the girls a joke. Happy New Year by the way."

Trudi moves closer to Buster, "He tried to put one on Athena."

"You dickhead, that's my girlfriend you're annoying.

Now, how about going away and leaving us alone. Or are we repeating yet again what we do every time we see you?"

I realise Buster is on his own. "Where are Nate and Artie? And the girls?"

"Those pussies didn't want to come, afraid of a summer storm. But, you know what, I came over to say hello, that's all. See you all around."

We all watch as he walks towards the surf club.

"That was easy," says Nigel, "I was more than ready to throw him one. Athena, are you ok?"

"Yeah, he was being a nuisance, that's all."

"Could have been worse if we weren't around though."

"Maybe, thanks for being around, Nigel." Athena kisses him, "You're my hero." Nigel puffs out his chest as he kisses her back.

The house is smaller than I expected, although I wasn't really sure what to expect. Sally lets me in as a yappy terrier accosts me. "Stop that, Bandit. Sorry, Edward, he'll calm down in a minute."

I follow her down a long hallway with bedrooms either side. Photos, family ones I think, line the walls on both sides. This opens into a kitchen and large dining area, floor to ceiling French doors opening out to a backyard flanked by two magnificent Jacarandas. So far it's a house similar to many in the area. I don't notice anything magical about it.

Sally's father and mother greet me warmly offering me a drink. "Go on outside, we're eating out there."

"Thanks Mr Thornton," I say holding my coke with lots of ice. Just how I like it, Sally must have told them that. Sally and I walk outside with Bandit following, he's calmed down now.

"Nice place." I had already told her parents what a lovely place they had. As we stand in the twilight of this warm evening, I realise Sally has grown this past year into a cute teen, I notice how mature she is.

"It's home, I don't know anything different. But thanks. So, how have the holidays been so far?"

I tell her how I'd been at the beach today and generally been doing that since school finished. It's where we hang out. I also tell her how Buster was there and basically did nothing other than say hello.

"Has he learned his lesson? Trying to be friendly now."

"Unlikely. He was on his own, Nate and Artie weren't around. Even though he hassled Athena and Trudi, he didn't try anything else. Without backup, he's a chicken."

"Ha, of course he is. Well, I'm glad he didn't ruin your afternoon."

"Dinner's ready," says Mr Thornton.

"Smells great, thanks for inviting me." We all settle down and enjoy the meal as we chat about the holidays, school and the three of them answer all my questions about magicals. They explain the animals in the meadow change with each meeting; the reason for the uniforms the 'royals' wear – it's a formal outfit they wear to meetings to distinguish them from the 'average' magical. I laugh at this.

"We have no hope of being anything like them," laughs Mrs Thornton along with me. "They are a special breed and do exceptional things with their magic. Speak to Ester about showing you the history books, they're stored in a safe at the A-Alliance house."

"I will, thanks. I have so much more to learn and want to do my best with the magic I've been given."

"You're doing well already, Edward. Keep listening and learning, I see great things for you."

I look at Mr Thornton wondering what he means but don't pursue it because it's time I left. "This has been great, thanks for dinner and the stimulating conversation."

"I'll see you out," says Sally. At the front door she says, "Thanks for coming, we rarely have visitors."

"Oh, my pleasure. Why not?"

"I'm not sure, but with no real friends at school, being the youngest magical at the Alliance, and no other family, it's pretty much only the three of us."

"Right. My place next time, I'd love you to meet my Mum. Although, she only knows about the cat thing…"

"Of course, I won't mention anything and that would be great."

"Great, I'll organise something before the holidays end." I leave heading for the bus station with a spring in my step.

THIRTY-ONE

Another School Year Begins

Term one flies by with little trouble from Buster and other bullies, mainly because along with Mr Ferris, we're all keeping a close eye on him and his crew. The girls, Stella and Beth had caused a stir a few weeks into the term when they bullied a popular girl, the Mayor's daughter. She had just started in Year 7. This was when we clamped down hard on any bullying because the Mayor had spoken with Mr Ferris and our Principal. She had threatened to take her daughter out of the school along with her friends, who were all from well-to-do families.

The school has tried to address the bullying issues, mainly with educational courses, but generally, it's up to us students to keep vigiliant.

Nigel and Athena are sitting in our usual lunch spot having a snog when I turn up. "Get a room you two."

"Jealous?" says Nigel. I am actually and it makes me think of Sally. We have seen each other a few times since the dinner. She met my mother, who liked her and was happy for me. I quickly explained we are only friends, but Mum gave me a wink, "Sure, if you say so." She had said this smiling.

I smile as Jackson and Trudi join us. Trudi still flirts openly with Jackson who ignores her in a polite way. He's a good guy, anyone else would have told her to shove it by now. Jackson had told me he didn't want to hurt her feelings, he would rather let her be as he is leaving at the end of the year. He had a trip to Europe planned.

We sit and have our lunch chatting about the usual crap – TV shows, sport, music and gossip. Lunch is over when an announcement crackles over the PA system.

"Everyone assemble in the quadrangle. Repeat. Assemble in the quadrangle."

We all look at each other shrugging and head to where we're told.

Our principal is on the balcony with Mr Ferris and the rest of the Staff. "We want to warn you of a cat-like creature prowling the suburb, possibly a panther. No one knows where this creature came from as the zoos haven't reported any missing animals. There has been a sighting in the back sports field and authorities have been alerted. We ask that you all calmly make your way to your lockers and then home. One year at a time, we don't want a stampede as this may alert the creature. Year 7, we will start with you."

We stand in our form year until our year is called. Trudi looks at me curious, her eyes wide. I shrug my shoulders, I have no idea what this creature is and what it's doing in suburban Sydney.

As soon as I'm home, my mother calls. "Are you ok, I heard some creature was prowling around your school?"

"We're all ok, I'm home. They let us come home early to keep us safe. And no, I don't know anything about the creature."

"Don't think about going out there as Milly, from what I

hear it's a panther or something like that, you wouldn't survive an attack."

"Mum, I'm not stupid. You take care coming home later, this thing could turn up anywhere."

"Ok, I love you. Stay home and safe."

"Love you too, Mum." After clicking off my phone, I go to my room and set up my laptop so I can comfortably speak to Sally.

The next day we're allowed to go to school as the creature was captured overnight. It was a panther, it had escaped from a private zoo a few suburbs away, the owner was a former zookeeper. Sally and I had spoken for hours last night after she had assured me it wasn't one of the magical creatures. "They wouldn't terrorise non-magicals," she had said. I walk in the school gates relieved this wasn't going to be another Leafia incident.

At my locker, Buster and his crew walk past. "Hey, Eddie, were you scared of the kitty cat." Buster turns his head smirking at me. So he is back to his old antics, but at least it's only words. I put my backpack on my shoulder heading out then I hear someone scream. As I walk out of the locker room I see Stella, she's on the floor bleeding from one knee.

Mr Ferris is already there. "Did you see where it went?" he asks Buster.

"Towards the back field, same as yesterday, I'd say."

"Ok, get Stella to the medical bay. I'll alert the authorities again."

"But the news said they caught it last night," says Bella.

"They did, this could be another one. Everyone get to your classrooms and stay there until further notice."

When I'm in my classroom I text Sally and she answers.

It could be Leafia, she can transform now. She might be angry about being banished.

How can the Alliance allow this to happen? Why isn't the banishment enforced?

Goblins can be fickle and become bored easily. When they have time on their hands, which they do when banished, they come up with schemes like this. She is probably copying what the real panther did, just for fun.

Fun! This is scaring the hell out of everyone, how stupid can she be? That's it, I have to do something. Talk later.

Edward, don't…

That's all I see of her last message as I transform into Milly.

I'm at the Jacaranda tree summoning up some strength, both mental and physical. If I'm going to help capture Leafia, I need all the help I can summon. Then I rush towards the back sports field that is swarming with rangers, teachers and police.

I can feel Leafia is close by and begin calling her. I'm speaking English but all anyone can hear is a meow. "Leafia, don't do this. Our magic is precious…" I continue trying to coax her out as I hear the rangers calling for the cat to be removed. "You'll be hurt, the rangers will shoot to kill," I continue. Then she answers.

"I was supposed to hurt that stupid bully but that girl was in the way. I should be helping you, I was banished before I could finish."

"Leafia, this is not the way. Leave here and we can discuss this at a meeting, I'm sure Ester will see reason and that you just want to help."

"She hates me and always has."

"Leafia, please stop this. The non-magicals have done nothing wrong." Before she can answer, I hear a loud growl and Leafia picks me up by the scruff of the neck as we become invisible. She heads for the school gates and when we're out of sight of everyone chasing us, we both transform.

"What the hell are you playing at?" We've ended up at the back of the park, in the bushland.

"Keep your voice down, we don't want to attract

attention. And lighten up, Edward, just having a bit of fun." Her shrill voice is hushed as she doesn't want us caught.

"Are you crazy? This is going to get us into so much trouble."

"The bullies are the ones who should be getting into trouble. Your principal and the rest of your teachers turn a blind eye to what they do, I was trying to highlight that."

I am angry beyond words and think about what our next step should be. "We need to get to the A-Alliance house, this needs to be fixed. The non-magicals saw the two of us as cats disappear into thin air."

"You're overthinking this, Ester can use that spell she used on Buster, they'll forget all about it."

"Leafia, it's not that simple, this was a crowd of people, not just one. Come on, let's go." I pull at her arm but she shrugs me off. She follows me anyway, which I'm grateful about because I was about to pick her up and carry her if she hadn't.

THIRTY-TWO

The Non-Magicals are Suspicious

The incident makes the news and our disappearing act goes viral because everyone had their phones out.

Ester is enraged and has summoned the magical committee. The dignitaries are all lined up at a bench, we're in a type of courtroom - dark timber chairs, alcoves and benches are all around us. Magicals are seated throughout the room murmuring about what Leafia has done.

A clap of Ester's hands quietens everyone. Leafia and I are at the front, standing facing the committee.

"Esteemed committee members, dignitaries, and magicals of the world. We appreciate your presence at this extraordinary meeting as we decide how to deal with this mess Leafia and Edward have caused." I think about protesting by placing my hand in the air, but quickly put it down when Ester glares at me.

"Leafia was banished, how did she come back?" asks Sally's father.

"Would you like to answer that, Leafia? We're interested to know."

"Ester, our esteemed chair, I came back to help. The bullies were going back to their usual antics, I couldn't stand back and watch Edward and his fellow geeks go through this again."

"It is not our place, Leafia. The non-magicals only require our assistance when absolutely necessary. Edward and his friends have done a brilliant job of cutting out bullying up till now. You are to be punished while we clean up your mess."

Everyone in the room begins clapping and cheering as Leafia protests. "With a spell you can fix this, you have already used one on Buster, just do it again."

"You young ones think everything is so simple," says Sally's father. "The crowd included rangers, police, teachers and students. Not to mention the media and internet, that is a lot of people we have to make forget."

"Make her do it."

"Leafia needs to make them forget."

"She needs to fix this."

Throughout the room, people are shouting and pointing at Leafia.

Ester claps again, the room silenced within seconds. "The committee will decide what is to become of Leafia." She continues to read from an enchanted book in front of her, a set of incantations in a language I don't recognise. Many repeat what Ester is saying, leaving me in awe and wondering what the hell is going to happen to Leafia and I.

Reporters are at the school gates again, they have been all week. They don't hassle us students, but the teachers and our principal are targeted.

"Tell us what you know?"

"We only need a minute of your time"

"Do you feel unsafe?"

Our principal had given a statement after the

disappearance guided by the police in what to say. Since then everyone had been asked to stay quiet.

Trudi and I walk in the gates with our heads down. Once we're out of earshot of the reporters she asks, "Don't you have any news about what happened?"

"Even if I did I wouldn't be able to discuss it with you. There are rules around magic, I've told you before. And I'd rather not talk about it now, there is still too much interest around what happened."

"Of course, everyone is suspicious of the two cats that disappeared in front of their eyes, this is not going away easily. You need to help stop this paranoia."

She's right, people are paranoid about what happened, the rumours of magical happenings are escalating, even though we magicals know nothing else has occurred. We walk in silence the rest of the way to our lockers and don't discuss it for the rest of the day.

Leafia is in my room when I return from school. "What are you doing here?"

"Apologising. I didn't think my little prank would get you in trouble too."

Dumping my backpack on my dresser, I throw myself on my bed. "Thanks but being banned from becoming Milly for three months is not such a burden for me. You're the one who has been given the real punishment. How's it going with getting around to everyone that needs to forget?"

"Slow. The incantation has to be done with the person present and I've been told to be careful in case my invisibility suddenly turns off. So, I'm doing a few people a day. I have asked Ester to find others to help out, she has agreed to allow others to cast the spell too because of the enormity, too many non-magicals for me to do it on my own."

Thinking that there should be a magic spell to work on groups rather than just individuals, I park this thought for another meeting of the A-Alliance. Sitting up on my left arm,

I look at Leafia who seems to be showing remorse for what happened. "It will take many months but has to be done. You seem sorry and won't do something so stupid again, right?"

"I'm not promising anything. Goblins are not bound by all the rules you magicals abide by. If I see the need to help, I will do so."

I sigh, "You are stubborn and my advice is you leave the bullies to us, Buster and his crew are our problem to fix. Mr Ferris has organised for them to take more courses on bullying prevention, our school has a non-bullying policy in place. All schools do."

"Sure, whatever you say. I have forgetting spells to cast, see you around, Edward." With this she disappears.

Lying back down on my pillow I think about what has happened. The paranoia is still rife, whispers abound about strange creatures in the dark with everyone scared. The bullying at school has decreased again, but for how long? I'm banned from helping now if Buster decides to start again. He is busy trying to change his ways by taking the courses Mr Ferris organised, let's hope he doesn't begin again before my three months are up.

Three months later, my penance is lifted. Ester has cautioned me to be careful and only use Milly when necessary. I promise to do my best and with the bullies silenced for some time now, I may not need Milly as much as before.

Sally and I are coming out of the movies, we're still only friends and enjoy each other's company, so hang out occasionally. "How about a milkshake?" She nods and we walk into the café next to the cinema.

We sit and generally chat about the past few months, the café is empty. We have discussed what happened often and now that the paranoia is almost over, the spells have been dispensed by many more magicals than just Leafia, it's safe to talk amongst other magicals again.

"Do you know what's happened to Leafia?" asks Sally.

"She's banned again, this time Ester and the committee has placed stronger bounds on her. I like her, but she can be a menace."

"That's goblins for you," laughs Sally as we slurp our milkshakes.

"How are things at your school? Mine has enforced a no tolerance to bullying."

"Yeah, we're pretty much the same. I don't think the courses did anything for Buster, but between us and the teachers, not just Mr Ferris now, we keep him and his crew under control."

She smiles, "You've done a great job, Edward, your sister would be proud." I look up from my drink and smile back.

"I couldn't have done it without her."

EPILOGUE

Ten Years On

I look around and smile at everyone here. This is a perfect sun-drenched November day and I'm sweating in my suit. Standing under the Jacaranda tree in this park is helping a little as I wipe my hand over my brow. I see Sally walking towards me after speaking with Anthea and Nigel, their two-year-old, Ailsa, in her pram.

"How are you doing, handsome?" asks Sally.

"It's a little warm," I reply as I take in my wife in her golden sheaf dress, her bump showing slightly. We only announced the pregnancy a few weeks ago, my mother is reeling with happiness. I look over at her sitting with other parents, including Sally's. My mum has been battling pneumonia that placed her in hospital for a week, but there was no way she was going to miss this wedding, like everyone she is curious to see the bride. Sally and I are the witnesses too, she couldn't have missed this either.

The marriage celebrant walks over and asks us to go to the

decorated rotunda resplendent in billowing white sheers and flowers, where the groom is waiting. I take Sally's hand and we walk to where Jackson is standing.

He smiles as we walk up to him. "These suits are not the most comfortable, are they?"

"Not in summer, no." I take in the worried look on his face. "Don't be nervous, she'll be here."

He looks at his watch, "She's fifteen minutes late, she's not usually late."

"It's a big day, Jackson," says Sally, "she wants to look perfect."

Jackson had returned from his gap year five years ago, a gap year that turned into five. He had the time of his life, working and living throughout England and Europe. While living in London, he met up with the love of his life again too.

When he came back home, he concentrated on studying and is now an architect. He and his partner had kept their promises of achieving degrees before settling down.

The other guests begin to take their seats, Jackson's parents at the front with his two brothers and their partners. People are chatting and greeting each other, as you do at weddings.

I remember our wedding day with fondness, we had opted for a winter's day at a wedding venue at the Great Lakes. Like this wedding, it was a small affair with only close family and a few friends, some of whom we've known since school. The only people missing were my father and Milly, but I felt them in spirit.

I'm shaken out of my reverie when a black car pulls up. The bride walks out in a glorious white gown dazzling with diamantes, her slim figure slivers as she moves in the dress, her unruly hair tamed into black silky straightness, and she has a huge smile on her face. Her father is on one side, her mother on the other.

When she arrives at where we are standing, her parents answer the celebrant that they are giving her away and she turns to Jackson, "Sorry I'm late." She gives him a light kiss on the cheek.

Trudi then turns to everyone and shouts, "Let's do this."
THE END

ACKNOWLEDGMENTS

When I sit down to write, I'm not always sure of the genre of the story. My stories take on a persona of their own, with this latest one, Edward's Cat, allowing me to follow the trials of a young boy as he navigates school while being bullied. This is not my first foray with Young Adult stories, I have one published as an eBook on Amazon – The Shop on the Princes Highway.

The idea for Edward's story started as a writing prompt for one of my writing groups, *Write on Water*. It is thanks to the other authors in that group that this story is now published. I thank you, especially those who helped with reading and editing, your suggested changes were invaluable.

I recommend any author, especially emerging ones, to join a local writing group. Follow them on socials too. The knowledge and camaraderie you receive is great. Our meetings are always full of facts, fun and sometimes food. We encourage each other and together we can achieve anything in this writing and publishing gig.

To my colleague and friend, Mark Drolc, for yet another fantastic cover design. You put up with my changes as well as my many ideas but you always deliver something sensational. Mark runs his own graphic design business and always finds time to help me out. A big thanks to you, Mark.

To my amazing friends who support me regularly, your friendship is also invaluable. And your encouragement has never wavered.

Of course, thanks go to my family, my husband Tony, our children and their partners, and our extended family. You're all behind me encouraging my creativity, and for this I'm grateful. Also, to my parents, who have no idea where this writing came from, but they are proud of my passion.

Edward's Cat is a novella, longer than a short story but not quite a novel. This doesn't make it any easier to write, but no less enjoyable. I hope you enjoy this story and look forward to any feedback, comments or ideas.

Happy reading,
   Maria P Frino

9 780648 894681